ELEVATED LUST

First Edition

Jardonn Smith

ELEVATED LUST

First Edition

Published by The Nazca Plains Corporation
Las Vegas, Nevada
2007

ISBN: 978-1-887895-73-6

Published by

The Nazca Plains Corporation ®
4640 Paradise Rd, Suite 141
Las Vegas NV 89109-8000

PUBLISHER'S NOTE
Elevated Lust is a work of fiction created wholly by *Jardonn
Smith's* imagination. All characters are fictional and any resem-
blance to any persons living or deceased is purely by accident.
No portion of this book reflects any real person or events.

Cover, Les Byerley
Art Director, Blake Stephens

ACKNOWLEDGEMENTS

To all the working men I've worked with and worked on.

ELEVATED LUST

Jardonn Smith

CONTENTS

FROM OUT OF NOWHERE

ROLL THE DICE

The landscape of the United States changed dramatically when gambling became legal in many cities and no longer was restricted to Las Vegas, Reno or Atlantic City. For me, it meant new opportunities to find horny men close to my home.

It had become my habit to book a weekend room at one of the new casinos on the outskirts of town. This particular establishment attracted me for two reasons. Number one, there was a truck stop nearby and many of the drivers would spend down time by gambling or eating at the casino restaurants; number two, the Pacific Diner served some of the best food for miles around at very reasonable prices. Designed like an eatery from a railroad depot in the 1940's, the place was always abuzz with hungry people, but spacious enough so that nobody ever had to wait for service. Better yet, the tables and booths were arranged so that everybody could see everybody no matter where they sat.

Normally, I would never pay much attention to groups of people, only solitary men, but on a particular Friday evening three male subjects were ushered to a table in the smoking section, and despite my best efforts I could not take my eyes off of them. They were seated about 15 feet from my booth and the one who most fit my profile just happened to notice my gaze. His eyes brightened just a bit and I could sense he made mention of me to his two companions, as the three of them engaged in conversation out of my hearing range.

My meal of pot roast had just been served, so I ate slowly and watched the waitress take their orders. Every time I'd glance up from my plate, at least one of them would be looking my direction. We played this game of me catching their stare and them catching mine until I nodded my head with a closed-mouth smile, soliciting a mimicked response from my favorite as though he recognized me, which of course he did not. Now all that remained for me to do was to casually work on my meal as they received theirs, and then drink my coffee and smoke a cigarette as they worked on their meal. This gave me plenty of time to decide on my opening line. When their plates were removed and they awaited their ticket, I left my money for the servers and strolled towards the exit by way of their table.

"Hey, you fellas drive for CFI Freight?"

"No, we came in from Larson."

They weren't truck drivers like I'd thought, but that didn't matter. The important thing is that the prize catch of this trio was the speaker and also seemed to be their ringleader, so I used a true story to further engage him.

"No kidding? Me and a buddy of mine follow the Silver Springs football team. We drove to Larson High School once to watch them play."

"You mean you watched them kick Larson's ass."

"Yeah, they do that to everybody they play. The Bulldogs have one hell of a team for small schools. It's why we leave the city to see them."

"Pull up a seat."

"So, do you guys go to the games?"

"Oh, sure. Harold here has a boy that plays." He pointed to the tallest of the group."Me and Kurt's got daughters on the cheerleading squad. In fact, that's where our wives went this weekend... takin' a bunch of the girls to a mini-camp up in Stockton."

"Oh, I see. So *that's* why you animals are on the loose."

They liked that. I could almost see their table rise when I said it.

"Yeah," answered the leader. "We're outta the cage for a coupla days.

I'm John. You wanna cup?"

I thought to myself, *Sure, John, I'll have a cup of your semen*, but instead I introduced myself. "Sure, John, I'll have a cup of your coffee. Hi, fellas, I'm Martin."

John motioned for their server to bring an empty cup for me and another full pot for the group. In succession, three cigarettes were lit by Harold, John and myself. Kurt didn't smoke. Kurt didn't care. All three of my hosts were about the same age and had a comfortable, easy-going demeanor, but I focused most of my attention on John, since he was the one who'd struck my fancy and also opened the door for our friendly chat. Do you want to know what we talked about? Football and farming, the latter of which I knew little, but I can be a good listener when the speakers make me horny.

All three were born on their families' farms, grew up and worked on those farms, and then took over the operations when their fathers decided they were old enough to do so. They had come to the city from their little town of Larson looking for excitement, so by the time our pot of coffee was emptied I had made it known to these men that I had a room upstairs and anytime they were ready, so was I.

Now, I don't want you to worry about me, so I'll let you in on a little secret. It is my custom to pack an extendable-bladed knife in my overnight bag for these types of adventures, and before going on the prowl I strategically hide this blade somewhere in the room where it is easily obtainable if such a need should arise. I have never used it, and on this night I had no qualms that these men were anything but ready to exploit their freedom. They were ready, with no hang-ups, no apprehensions, and frankly I suspected that they had diddled one another back in the days when they first discovered that their young dicks could play new tricks. So forget about drama. Let's put our minds at ease and have some fun. That's what I did.

Open entering my room, the top priority was to unload that coffee from my bladder, and one by one, Kurt, Harold and John did the same. In the middle of the room was a king size bed. While Kurt pissed, we three peeled the covers down to the floor. I made sure ashtrays were on the bedside tables and left one lamp lit. That's all the artificial illumination we would require.

Since Kurt was my first guest to get himself freshened up, I strolled over to him and unbuttoned the top of his shirt. "Whatcha got under there?"

He immediately pulled the shirt tail out from his jeans and unfastened all buttons. It was Harold's turn in the bathroom and John, who stood nearby, proceeded to lift his pocket t-shirt over head while giving his buddy some encouragement. "Might as well strip down, Kurt. We're gonna be here awhile."

Within seconds, Kurt had pulled off both western boots, dropped his jeans and removed his white socks. For a second or two he stood upright and winked at me, then unashamedly yanked down his briefs, stepped out of them and flung himself onto the bed flat. Kurt laid on his back with arms and legs sprawled, his flaccid penis resting comfortably on his gonads. With John playing spectator from the corner foot of the bed, I crawled onto the mattress, knelt between Kurt's thighs and delicately lifted his cock using one thumb and one finger. Into my mouth he went.

Kurt was an average looking guy when dressed. Much better naked. Aren't they all? On his chest was a thin patch of dark brown hair, a narrow line extending onto his stomach before exploding with thickness below his belly button. Here, his fur widened into a wiry mesh with his curly pubic hair, which rarely if ever had been trimmed. No matter, my wet lips and warm, scraping tongue brought his cock out of the bushes. Its emergence dramatically filled my mouth to confirm that his dick was the perfect length and width for sucking on. Easily serviced without breaking one's jaw.

Whereas the man on the mattress had nothing to say, the other two bantered behind me.

"Man," John made his way for the toilet. "Thought you'd never get outta there."

"You better hurry up," Harold came out relieved. "Looks like we're off and running."

Sounds made earlier by Kurt were repeated by Harold. There were boots hitting the floor, belt unbuckling, snap unsnapping, zipper unzipping and fabric peeling from skin. One minute later, Harold joined us and positioned himself behind me. My jeans were poked, and I don't mean with a finger.

I suppose it was selfish of me, but by this time I was getting my jollies with the cock in my mouth and figured I'd just let Harold fend for himself. Testing the boundaries, I laid the palms of my hands onto Kurt's belly and felt its hard surface. There was no protest. His eyes were closed. He smiled with satisfaction, so I hand-rubbed his chest and belly while continuing to mouth-stroke his meat. Ruggedly solid. This was Kurt. Not bulked up but naturally strong, a body built from hard work. Feeling him while sucking on him created a problem for me, as my own peter tried its best to find an escape route, a problem which Harold now addressed.

He unbuckled my belt, and then opened my jeans from snap to zipper. With John's emergence from the bathroom, I decided that perhaps I should try to be a more welcoming host. I kindly left Kurt's erection laying on his belly and set about to making my guests more comfortable. "Looking for a poke, are you, Harold?"

"Thought I might."

"Hold on a second and I'll get you set up."

I headed for the bathroom, took another piss and cleaned myself up, then grabbed a bunch of towels and a bottle of my baby oil. After dumping everything onto the bed, I proceeded to strip down while John stood nearby watching the festivities.

Gazing upon his shirtless body, I saw everything I'd hoped for. Thick and sturdy, short and stout, the first thing to strike me was the fact that his laterals were flared to such a degree that his arms were forced to angle outwards, even when hanging unused. He was strong as an ox and the upper torso was more than impressive, but I noticed he wasn't removing any more of his wardrobe, so I asked him. "Well, John, ready to jump in here?"

He grinned and scraped his chest with the tips of his fingers. "Nah, I think I'll watch you fellas for awhile. Gets me hard just seeing my buddies bust a nut."

I wasn't sure how I felt about the best-looking man hovering in the background while I serviced those buddies of his, but figured he'd come around when the time was right for him. He'd better. If it wasn't for John I'd probably never have gone after the other two in the first place, but they were ready and waiting and certainly pleasing enough for my eye, so I got busy.

My dick was free to wag and dribble, so I got back between Kurt's thighs, taking a gander at Harold before restarting Kurt's patient pecker. Harold was a stark contrast to the other two men. Tall and lanky, Harold's body was thin but handsomely chiseled, again the result of hard labor. His fingers, hands, feet and toes were long and slender in conjunction with his penis, which he proudly stroked in his baby-oiled palm while kneeling erect on the mattress next to Kurt's right shin.

I knew that soon he'd be impaling me deep and hard, but my focus remained directed to the surrendered man below. Positioning myself on all fours with hands on either side of Kurt's hips, I left my buttocks at a convenient height for Harold to do his thing while I turned up the intensity on the meat in my mouth. Kurt responded, lost in his fantasy. Comfortable exhales mumbled words and sounds of satisfaction, such as "Mmm" or "Oh yeah" or others that typographical symbols can't define, especially when I'd crush the head of his tool in the back of my throat. Since I liked his sounds, I made this a habit every time he was caught on my down stroke.

Harold made good use of my baby oil. The gentle soul lubricated the rim of my ass with his oily fingers before pressing his rod against me. With my knees outside of Kurt's, I spread mine a bit further and nudged Kurt's with my hands so he would open up, too. Harold was given a wide berth, both on the mattress and between my butt cheeks. Gaining entry with an easy and steady thrust, he lingered a few seconds in waiting for me to loosen up a bit, and then probed his way into me deeper and deeper until I felt his pelvic bone pressing against my butt cheeks.

Harold was mine. Or I guess I was his, depending on how you feel about it. I felt like he was mine, because my ass-muscled clamp onto him was equal to my throat-muscled clamp onto Kurt, but whereas Kurt surrendered to me trance-like, Harold dominated me man-like. One oily hand and one dry clutched my hips. Harold slowly speared and retracted, swiveling his pelvis to attack from another angle. He poked from left, right, above and below, gradually increasing his pace, markedly intensifying his force. His deepest penetration received the warm vise of my strong scrotum clinch. I dared him to retract, fighting him to stimulate him, while matching his pace into me with my pace onto Kurt. The three of us focused one hundred percent on our task and little by little increased the pleasure of our ecstatic exercises.

The sounds of three men morphed into grunts of animal lust, interrupted by the sparking flint of a lighter. Smoke filled the air, courtesy of a John-fired cigarette. His form came into my left view. He was stalking us, still with jeans but shirtless, as he took a seated position near Kurt's chest. "God damn, Kurt. You're gettin' quite a workout."

Eyes opened and Kurt turned his head. "Yeah, Johnnie, this fella knows what he's doin', that's for sure."

With cigarette in one hand, John rubbed his own chest with the other before transferring that hand to Kurt's chest. He massaged with his palm, scraped a nipple with his thumb while grinning at Harold. "Hey, you still with us back there? You're working up a sweat, big man."

Harold was busy thrusting and grunting. I was busy clamping and stroking. Kurt was busy moaning and writhing, and as John moved off the bed and out of sight we all three forgot about him. At least I did, until I felt a rough hand encircle my penis. I was manually stroked by a man who could not be forgotten, the man who instigated this fiasco to begin with.

And such a thoughtful man, too, I thought to myself. Those scratchy fingers of John's focused on the head of my dick were just what I needed to finish the other two. Manly grunts came from the man behind me, as helpless moans wafted up from the man beneath. Kurt tensed his body and jettisoned a foamy cream into my mouth, while Harold poked and prodded at an increasingly frantic pace. Just then, John's fingers transformed from scratchy to slick, a result of baby oil squirted to lubricate his pump.

"C'mon, Martin. Shoot that baby," he encouraged.

This move by John benefitted Harold as much as it did me, because my scrotum clenched with power to crush the cock in my ass. Poor guy. Harold groaned as though some burly wrestler was crushing him in a bear hug. His dick couldn't help but fire its load. It was the only way out of my grip. With Kurt on the come-down, his semen drained and swallowed, Harold slammed himself against my butt cheeks time and again, scraping and shooting rapid fire. His groaning, grunting and near collapse onto my spine confirmed his explosion, which left only me and John with nuts still bulging. Mine were on the verge of losing their bounty, but until they did Harold and Kurt were going nowhere. I crushed Harold in my rectum; I squeezed Kurt in the back of my throat, sending post-orgasmic ripples of pain and pleasure from their heads to their toes.

Now, it was up to John. As I kept my prisoners contorting, his hard-surfaced but tempered-with-oil fingers frantically squeezed and stroked the head of my cock. His rough hand on my dick was joined by four more at other places, as Harold collapsed onto my back with his arms wrapped around my belly and Kurt uselessly tried to control me by clutching his fingers into my trapezius muscles.

Masculine fingers, working-man hands, the best of which belonged to John, the man who drove me nuts, all combined to drain my nuts. Unholy spurts of my sticky jizz splattered to the mattress sheet below me. Correction: it saturated the hand towel John had smartly placed atop the sheet beneath my chest and belly. What seemed an impromptu decision to take care of my problem was actually a pre-planned expression of mutual gratification. This man, this farmer named John, liked what he'd seen and made sure I knew about it. My admiration for him suddenly bordered on dangerous.

NEXT VICTIM?

Seems I had rustled up a very talented group of men. Harold's softening dick gently slipped past the rim of my asshole, Kurt's comfortably flopped onto his belly when released from my lips, while mine continued basking in John's finishing squeezes. The final move was his, and once satisfied that all my semen had oozed and dropped, John lifted the towel and dabbed my slit. "That was quite a show," John congratulated all of us. "Three rockets firing at the same time... helluva thing."

We untangled. Harold and I reached for some towels to remove the baby oil from our peckers; John found a chair and plopped; Kurt did nothing. He laid sprawled and motionless with eyes closed, nearly dozing until John started to razz him.

"Hello, Kurt... are you still with us? Come in, Kurt."

"Heck of a deal, Martin," Kurt ignored John in order to praise me. "You're a top-notch pro... great BJ." He rolled off the bed and disappeared into the bathroom.

With Harold and I sitting on the mattress, we all three lit up our smokes while I queried John. "Well, everybody's been satisfied except you. What's your pleasure?"

"I'll just wait for you guys to go at it again. Kinda liked seeing that."

I looked at Harold and he rolled his eyes, which caused my heart to frustratingly sag. The idea that John's only interest was to watch us certainly put a damper on the exhilaration of five minutes earlier. I refused to accept it, but for now would have to be content with what I'd accomplished so far. Besides, none of them were giving indications that they were in a hurry to be anywhere other than with me, so I was far from defeated.

"Ok, John, but I'm afraid you'll have to wait awhile for your eyewitnessing. Don't know about your two buddies, but I need a little rest period."

"I'll bet you do."

Kurt's return put three naked men on the bed and one semi-clothed man, John, in his distant chair by curtain-drawn windows, jeans and stocking feet keeping half of him a mystery. We cycled through several cigarettes and trips to the toilet, plus in between took short swigs from the bottle of bourbon I had brought with me. Everybody was warm and happy and totally comfortable, but when John finally took his turn in the bathroom I dug for information.

"What does he like to do?"

"Like he said," Harold answered. "He's a watcher."

"Doesn't he like to get his dick sucked?"

"Nope. Says it's just a bunch of slobberin'. Doesn't want anything to do with the anus, neither. Just likes pussy, I guess."

Kurt joined in. "All we've ever done is given him dry hand jobs way back when. He liked that, but it was a long time ago."

"Hand job?" I laughed at this. "Hell, he can do that himself. Bet I could change his way of thinking. What do you say, Kurt? Think I could?"

Harold interrupted. "Sorry, Martin. You can't make a dog eat cat food."

Bullshit, I said to myself. "Sure you can," I said to them. "Just put it out there and the dog will eat." Kurt chuckled and Harold shook his head, while I probed for anything that might persuade our voyeur that better things were waiting. "Well, maybe at least we can get him down here on the bed with us. I'd kinda like to touch some body parts. Think he'd mind that?"

"Might work. We'll see."

This scenario was frustrating me pretty good. After all, who ever heard of a man not wanting to get his dick sucked? I figured probably some woman (perhaps his wife) had done a sloppy job on him at one time or another, which would explain his negative attitude. Maybe that wasn't at all the reason for John's peculiar reluctance, but it was motivation for me. The night was young. His presence drove me crazy. If I could just get an opportunity to put my touch to him, if he could know that Kurt's praise of me was genuine, then he'd alter his opinion real quick. We'd just wait and see who did what to whom.

Unbeknownst to me, my stressing over this situation was no longer necessary. Plotting was afoot, not by me, but by Harold and Kurt. Both stared downward, lost in thought, as my obvious disappointment and recently-exhibited skills set their minds to thinking of ways to trick John. They'd felt what I could do and they fully intended for John to take advantage of his opportunity whether he wanted to or not. With John's opening of the bathroom door, Harold and Kurt began to reminisce.

"Hey, Kurt, you remember the summers we used to make extra money putting up hay?"

"Sure. Marcum's, Johnson's and uh... the Bickelmeyer place."

"And don't forget Hoover's. One right after the other. Had to do 'em all in four weeks."

"Yep. We'd work like dogs all day long, hot as hell out there in the fields."

"Yeah, but we were youngsters then. Didn't faze us one bit. Best part I recall was the naked cool downs in ol' man Hoover's pond."

John stood at the foot of the bed with hands on hips, as though he knew these two were up to no good.

"Oh, yeah," Kurt continued. "Every day when the sun'd go down, we'd strip for a dip."

"Which would always lead to a wrestling match in the shallows." Harold reached up and poked John in the stomach. "Remember those days, Johnnie-boy?"

Do you want to know how you can tell you're in the presence of a real man? When Harold's finger was thrust into John's gut, John didn't even flinch. So confident was he in his naturally powerful defenses, John felt no need to tighten his already solid muscles. Instead, he just grunted and disgustedly added his part to the flashback. "Yeah, you sons-a-bitches would gang up on me. Not that it did you any good. I'd whip both of you. Remember?"

"That's true, except for the times when you'd let us win." Evil defined the facial expressions of Harold and Kurt; red-faced embarrassment defined John's.

"Shit. I only let you win 'cause I knew you two'd drag me up on the bank and jack me off."

Harold jumped up and stood behind John. "That's right. Hey, Kurt, does this look familiar?" He put a full-nelson onto the shirtless man and pulled back his arms. "I'd bring him outta the water and get him on top of me, then you'd jack that fat pecker of his."

"Well, get him outta the water and let me at him." Kurt jumped off the bed and so did I, taking a seat in the chair well out of their way. Joining his partner, Kurt guided Harold to turn around, still holding the unresisting John in his full-nelson. He flopped, landing with back on the mattress and John on top of him. Their four legs dangled off the foot of the bed, Harold's bare feet nearly touching the floor, John's stocking feet several inches above and in between Harold's.

My heavenly side-view instantly brought me an erection. John's wide, muscular chest rose high into the air, as Harold stretched John's arms down towards him. John offered no resistance, instead pretending to protest by turning his head side to side. His exaggerated inhales and exhales further dramatized his powerful chest and thick-meated, hard-walled belly, as it dropped like a cliff from the end of his rib cage. His legs never moved when Kurt removed his socks, but as his belt was unbuckled, jeans unsnapped and zipper lowered, he raised his head with lower jaw extended, groaning a feigned request for pity. "Oh, no... what are you doing to me?"

He helplessly watched Kurt tug his jeans away from him. First from one leg and then the other, little by little the denim was removed until completely past his ankles and heaped on the floor. John was left with nothing but his white briefs for protection. "Oh, my god... no." John dropped his head into the crook of Harold's shoulders, awaiting his fate.

I also awaited his fate, patiently and excitedly. Three grown men had stepped into a time warp, returning to days of their youth at Hoover's pond. Hearing John say those words, plus seeing him stretched in that torturous position brought me into the fantasy with them. There's something about a man stripped to basic white briefs that is mysteriously tantalizing. Every inch of him is exposed except for the organ that defines him, and even though you can visualize what it might look like, you can only see the outline. What's hidden and unknown can be almost as exciting as having the damned thing in full view. With great effort, I kept my hands away from my own dick to critique their play.

Kurt reached inside John's underwear, grabbed his hidden pecker and pumped it with his fist. John groaned, then sighed painfully pleasured, as Harold issued a softly-spoken threat. "You ready to give up? Or do we gotta beat you some more?"

"I'll never give up."

"Then we'll have to work you over 'til you do."

And with that, Kurt yanked John's briefs all the way to the floor, forcing me to rise from my chair and assume the role previously performed by John – content to hover, content to watch, thrilled to inspect.

Short and stocky, John was built solid as a fireplug. Strong-ass son of a bitch had a big, barreled chest with wide pectorals and the aforementioned expanding laterals; hard belly with plenty of lines and curves, plus a deep ridge running from the pit of his stomach to his navel to his pubic hair. A long line of fur between his pelvic bone and his rounded, slightly inset navel begged to be licked, as did the thick muscle underneath. His exaggerated exhales and flexing of that belly challenged me to do just that, but I couldn't, so I looked away, waiting for Harold and Kurt to do their thing. Oh, and speaking of fur, his upper torso was painted with dark brown hair on his chest, belly and arms – not the long and heavy kind, but the short and soft kind – the type and amount of body hair that enhance the beauty underneath without dominating the overall effect.

And here he was totally surrendered with his wrists parallel to his ears and arms pulled down towards the mattress. Harold's torso lay underneath, which forced John's powerful chest high into the air and caused his belly to flatten with every muscle highlighted for me to enjoy.

John's cock disappeared into the clutches of Kurt's right hand. Standing between Harold's and John's spread apart legs, Kurt gently pumped John's meat a few times, and then stroked the middle while rubbing his thumb on that sensitive triangle where corona meets shaft.

With a slight lifting of his legs John responded to Kurt's touch. He raised his head, peered over his chest and juxtaposed a verbal "you rotten bastard" with a satisfied grin that said continue. His leg lift nearly did me in. The muscles in his belly exploded to life, three heavy lines on each flank pointing to his deep-ridged center, the knot of his belly button rising to peer out of its dark hole, and it took every ounce of will power for me to resist burying my face into that thing right then and there.

Fortunately, Kurt moved things along. "Looks like we will have to beat you down." His left hand formed a fist and plowed into John's stretched belly with medium force, hard enough to cause a deep-thudded smack.

"Uh, you pussy. Is that all you got?" No, it wasn't. Kurt landed another punch, same spot, directly over the navel. Did John defend himself? Not really. His legs dangled, never moving. His hard abdominal wall efficiently absorbed the blow and he remained defiant. "Go ahead. I can't even feel it."

"Some fellas never learn." Kurt let go of John's dick. "Come on, Harold. Time to teach him a lesson."

Harold rolled to his left and released John's arms. He laid on his chest motionless as though sleeping, his knees at the foot edge of the mattress with calves and feet in midair angling towards the floor. As Harold left the bed, taking the pillows with him and tossing them onto the floor, Kurt grabbed John's ankles and flipped him onto his back, once again centered on the bed. He moved to the side of the bed to John's right and took his wrist. Harold, on the other side of the bed grabbed John's left wrist and together they dragged him towards the headboard. John was perfectly centered, spread eagled, his legs angled to corresponding foot posts and arms towards the head. They climbed onto the mattress and knelt beside his chest, Harold to John's left and Kurt to his right.

John did nothing. His eyes were closed, his body relaxed, except for the throbbing peter bouncing on his belly.

Harold took his turn driving a few punches to the pit of John's stomach. He still did nothing. His legs never moved. Kurt dropped two forearm smashes across John's expanded chest. All he got was a manly "Ugh" from his victim.

"What do you think we oughtta do with him?" Harold wanted to know.

"You got me." Kurt threw some of his own medium-strength punches into John's hard belly. "There's gotta be some way to break him down."

"He's hard as a rock. We'll never break him down this way." Harold pointed to the chest beneath them, "But I think I know of a soft spot. Let's see if he remembers this."

"Gonna rack him?"

"Damned right."

From my corner foot view I could see it all. Horny boys hard at work and hard at play. Old fantasies came to life, as Harold and Kurt maneuvered to lay on their sides and rest on one elbow. Each man slid one hand under John's back. In unison, they placed the tips of their tongues onto his nipples. His entire body tensed as though shocked with a jolt of electricity.

"Oh my god, you guys... Not that... anything but that." John raised his head and looked first to his right nipple, then his left. "You sick mother fuckers." With a mighty groan of surrender, John collapsed into this forgotten fantasy. His body writhed, as the simultaneous attack of his tormentors included licking with wet tongues and squeezing with dry lips. In between, Harold interjected phrases from their youthful past.

"Give up, tough guy... it's all over for you now."

"Uhh... never." He raised his head with lower jaw extended and challenged them. "Go ahead. Do your worst." His glazed eyes rolled upwards before he closed them and lowered his head to the mattress, surrendering to the fantasy.

With his free left hand, Harold punched John's gut. With his free right hand, Kurt pounded his chest. John never moved, not his legs, not his arms. They were in bondage or so it seemed, maybe chains, maybe ropes, but whatever he imagined his restraints to be, John defended himself solely with muscle, his penis being the only appendage reacting to their attack. "Oh, god damn... why are you doing this to me? I will whip both your asses... first chance I get."

He probably could have if he'd wanted to. John was stronger than all three of us put together, but that's what made this wild fantasy all the more tantalizing. For his defiance, Kurt and Harold rewarded him by raising his chest with their hands from underneath, further stretching his tits. They buried them into their mouths, sucking away on John's nipples like they were baby bottles. He moaned. His toes curled, and I could swear his fat cock grew another quarter inch. Uncontrollable contractions bounced his weapon on his hard belly, a sticky syrup spitting from its mouth to dot his skin and hair with shiny splotches.

As they worked him over, I paced from one side of the bed to the other like a caged animal, stopping at advantaged angles to take in the view. John's body and the things they were doing to it was a sight to behold, and as their assault upon his tits intensified, John's surrendered and relaxed response progressed to a state of elevated ecstasy. His chest expanded and he sucked in his belly as though trying to break free of his imaginary chains. His head lifted on occasion, his lower jaw thrust forward. He'd look to the left and right, watch them torture his nipples, snarl, grunt and drop back to the mattress, allowing them to continue. From the foot of the bed his tits could be seen underneath those merciless tongues and lips, their tips rising as their surface skin contracted to tiny brown dots.

As I listened to his exhaling groans, watched his flexing muscles and bouncing cock, a softly scraping sound came from below. His toes were curling back and forth. Were they waving at me? Demanding attention in their restraining irons of torture? I knelt on the floor at the end of the bed, frantically waving my hands to get someone's attention, and it was Kurt who interrupted his tit sucking with a smile and a nod to my pointing finger.

Using both hands, I formed a ring around each of John's ankles and gently pulled him towards me, further stretching his body. He groaned. I wrapped my fingers over the top of each foot and placed my thumbs onto his thick arches. Starting with a light touch, I rubbed up and down the entire surface from John's heels to the balls of his feet, where I applied a bit more pressure. Next, I used my forefingers and thumbs, grabbed hold of the skin between his big and second toes and gave that skin on both feet a gentle pinch. He raised his head with eyes glazed. John smiled at me, glanced at both mouths sucking on him, and then collapsed back to the mattress. "Uhhh, god damn, you guys are driving me nuts."

None of us answered, but instead continued our assault. I repeated my pinching technique between every one of his toes, then stood up and rubbed the soles of both feet. One at a time, I grabbed the tiny hairs on the tops of his toes and gave a gentle tug. John didn't look, but whispered an airy sigh. "Jesus H. Christ."

I crawled onto the foot of the mattress to begin my slow progression. Starting with his shins and massively muscular sides of his calves, I warmed his skin with rapidly paced hand rubs, occasionally squeezing the calves, occasionally tugging the bristled hair of his legs. His left, and then right leg were thoroughly explored, as I made my way towards the ultimate target.

After rubbing and squeezing his knees and thighs, my hands drifted towards his crotch. With a quick move, I took his throbbing, neglected peter into one hand and brought it straight down between his thighs, and then held it there while lowering my body on top of it. All my apprehensions vanished. John no longer was with us. His eyes were closed, his only head movement side to side, his only sounds ecstatic moans. We, or more to the point, I was free to do as I pleased.

With his dick secured under my chest, I rested both elbows onto the bed at either side of John's hips and put my lips to his middle section. Gingerly, I planted dry kisses from the pit of his stomach to his navel to his pubic hairs, where I reversed direction and retraced my path.

Initially, he sucked in and tensed his abdomen, then relaxed and breathed normally – heavily, but normally. With each dry lip contact, I pressed down a bit more, soon incorporating my nose and chin into my abdominal assault. John's skin was smooth and the hairs of his belly tickled my nose, but just below the surface I could feel the incredible power of this man. No matter how hard I buried my face into him, his abdominal wall did not budge.

While the two men above kept him occupied with their tantalizing tit torment, which now included free-hand massages to his elevated chest, I lavished further praise on his belly by bringing my wet tongue into play. Alternating between lips and tongue, I soon had his manly hairs moistened with tiny beads of spit and I could feel his helpless cock surging underneath me. All that pre-orgasmic syrup on his belly was removed. My appetizer tasted like a man.

For the first time in a long time somebody said something. It was John. His voice was deep, airy, anguished. "Uhhhh, you're torturing me."

He was primed, surrendered. I probably could have stuck my finger up his ass and he wouldn't have cared, but with Kurt's mouthing of the words "Finish him," I did what every good cock sucker should do

– introduced him to the world of the world-class.

Raising up, I took his cock into my hand and held it vertical, then wrapped my lips around the rim of his corona. My hand let go. There would be no hand-jobs for this man's dick tonight, or ever again if I had my say. With my palms planted firmly to the mattress on either side of John's hips, I swallowed every ounce of my spit before proceeding with mouth opened wide. My upper lip kept his cock standing vertical, as I lowered my head until the head of his cock touched the back of my throat. With one mighty chomp, I shut my jaw and clamped the entire length of his fat organ between my tongue and roof of mouth.

He jolted. The shock brought a pained "Uhh" of sudden ecstasy, as another charge of electricity raged through him. His back arched. He forcefully stretched his limbs in four directions as I slowly ascended his pole, my tongue wrapping his shaft as though a sausage in a bun.

As I scraped my way back towards his crown, I took care to swallow frequently and keep my mouth as dry as possible. Once my lips reached the rim of his mushroom, I brought it towards his feet, keeping it firmly held in my oral vise. Then, I reached back to clasp both hands around his ankles and pushed them towards the end of the bed, further stretching him on his rack. The fat meat of his dick pressed onto the tops of his balls, compressing them, causing their bull-like roundness to flare on either side of his bent shaft. I released his ankles and lightly scraped his sensitive-skinned nuts with my nails. John widened his legs, further exposing his semen-compressed testicles for me to scratch. Every exhale of his breath brought deep-throated and airy moans, as I kept his hard cock horizontally pressing his nuts to unleash my baby-bottle suck.

From midway on his shaft to his mushroom head is where my mouth stayed. With five or six short strokes, I sucked on the head of his tortured unit like I was extracting frozen and malted milk from a straw – a thick, powerful and pulsating straw, until I felt contractions and the room went silent. We had him so primed that he was instantly ready to shoot. Every muscle tensed to capacity and he arched his back with an incredible explosion of manly seed. My mouth was flooded, as I continued to hold his dick straight down over the tops of his frantically-finger-scratched nuts and suck his pulsating mushroom like a man possessed. While he shot his load, I continued to ruthlessly scrape with tongue and roof of mouth while gradually moving my head towards his belly, until his still-pumping organ was once again vertical and free to release its bounty in an unrestricted flow.

Such a beautiful tool this was, so perfectly suited for oral service that I longed to worship it for hours, longed to keep on attacking him until he gave me a back-to-back firing, but I feared that tormenting him with post-orgasmic pain and pleasure might be pressing our luck. He had been thoroughly drained by my talented mouth, so the point was made. As his writhing contortions ended, as Harold and Kurt removed their mouths from his nipples, I brought John's still-hard but non-contracting penis towards his belly, opened my lips and gently let him drop.

Nobody said a word. Kurt and Harold hand-rubbed his chest and belly, while I climbed off the bed, trying to pretend like what had just happened was no big deal. But it was a big deal. As John laid in his racked position, breathing heavily with eyes closed, we three perpetrators looked at one another with expressions of triumph, fully convinced we'd brought John something he had long forgotten. Together, we had taken him back to the days of his youth and I do believe, based on the volume of come I had just swallowed, that this was possibly the most satisfying orgasm he had experienced since those early days of discovery. And if there was any doubt remaining as to how John felt about it, he suddenly broke out of his afterglow to erase those doubts.

"Where the hell did you learn to do that?" John raised up to a seated position, casting his buddies aside.

"Dunno, John." I stood near the chair preparing to light a cigarette. "I guess the better the cock the better the cock sucker." I grabbed a smoke from his pack and lit two at once, handing his to him.

"What time is it?" Harold wanted to know.

"About midnight," I told him, as John laid down to recuperate.

Kurt piped in. "Well, I've got cattle to feed in the morning. Maybe we ought to wrap this up and head on home."

"Me, too. Better piss first, though." Harold made his way to the bathroom while Kurt got dressed, and then they reversed activities, failing to notice that John wasn't moving. With a curling finger, he had silently motioned for me to join him on the bed, and as I rested on one elbow positioned between his thighs to finger-rub his nuts, John made an announcement to his friends.

"I ain't goin' nowhere. You two can take care of my shit, can't ya?"

They looked at one another a bit stunned, but quickly accommodating. "Sure, John, we can do that. When do you want us to come and get you?"

"Guess Sunday afternoon oughtta be good enough. The women ain't comin' back 'til about six, or so they said. Check my recorder while you're there, too. You got this room number?"

"No. What is it?"

Since I had no inclination to interfere. I told them room 406 and John continued his instructions.

"Call and let me know if she's left any messages or anything else I oughtta know. We ain't goin' nowhere. Ain't that right, Martin?"

Feeling pretty good about these developments, I'd put out my cigarette and maneuvered myself onto my chest, laying between his legs with my lips snacking on those bull-sized nuts of his. "Uh... yeah," I answered between tasty ball munching. "*Umm... mumm...* sure, John... *umm... god damn... ummum... fuckin' monsters... umm...* whatever you say, John."

"Key ring's in my left pocket. Don't wreck my god damn truck, neither."

And that's how they left us. You think I didn't lick on his balls until they were ready to explode? For that matter, I licked every part of him I could get to. He let me, you know. Never moved. Didn't even bother getting a pillow, just sprawled himself out like before and let me go at him. I asked him if his tits were sore. He said it was nothing he couldn't handle. Tough-ass son of a bitch took everything I could give him, and I took that fat cock of his right up my ass while he laid there letting me do all the work. Mother fucker was an animal. Fired his load into my mouth or my ass every time I came calling. For two solid days I worked him over, slept with him for a couple of hours at a time before starting in again. I gave him my cigarettes when he ran out of his own, let him help me drink my whiskey, let him go to the bathroom whenever he needed, rode down the elevator with him to the diner when we were hungry, but the rest of the time we stayed naked while my tongue, hands, lips and ass were all over him. John took it like some sort of super-charged, teenaged stud, but believe you me, farmer John is all man.

I never prowl the Pacific Diner any more. I sit there waiting for John to join me for dinner. He calls to set up our weekend date about once a month. He comes alone, and our marathons keep me satisfied until he's ready to go at it again.

What I thought were three horny truck drivers turned out to be three good ol' boys from the middle of nowhere, and the one I wanted most – farmer John – ended up being the man who wanted me. I don't miss Kurt or Harold, but I do have fond memories of them. After all, without those two I never would have got to John in the first place. Because his buddies stirred up the past, and because my natural-born talents are elevated when he's on my bed, John performs for me like a testosterone-raging he-man. That's exactly what he is.

C.O.E.
(COOPERATIVE OCCUPATIONAL EDUCATION)

PART ONE – YOU'RE HIRED

"Holy crap, that feels good."

Those were the first words he said when I put his dick into my mouth. His arms were clamped defensively to his sides as he lay on my bed stiff as a board. He stared at the ceiling, fearful to look elsewhere, fearful that visual confirmation of what was happening to him would ruin the sensations created for him. In other words, what he said was motivation for himself, not me, but fortunately for both of us I knew what I was doing. My novice closed his eyes and gradually accepted what he felt. His body relaxed and very shortly thereafter he spoke once again, this time to signal his coming eruption. "Ah, geez... oh, yeah!"

And with that I drank a healthy dose of youthful semen.

Robert came to me by way of the *Cooperative Occupational Education* program at Winchester High School, which was run by a teacher named Henry Wilson. Mr. Wilson had sent young men to me before, usually between 15 and 17 years old, and those I had hired were always intelligent, dependable and willing to learn. Therefore, when teacher Wilson called to see if I had a position for one of his students, I cheerfully accepted. Once I saw the young man in question, he was as good as hired.

The job was simple enough. I was the warehouse manager in a little neighborhood department store. During the day, my staff would stock the warehouse shelves with incoming merchandise, then load the items onto wheeled carts which were to be distributed throughout the store in their appropriate departments. Most of this distribution took place late afternoons until the night-time closing at nine o'clock. This was the function of my student hires.

The interview was scheduled at four pm on a Friday and when I approached my little office at five minutes before, this youngster was waiting outside the door.

"Robert?"

"Yes, sir. Robert Flynn."

"Hello, Robert Flynn, I'm Matthew Russell. Mr. Wilson spoke well of you." I held out my hand and we shook. "Let's step in here and do some paperwork."

I got an application for him to fill out and ran a quick, conversational character test.

"Now Robert, I'm depending on you to eventually supervise yourself, because most nights you'll be the only one back here. I need you to be a trustworthy person. You will be responsible for watching thousands of dollars' worth of merchandise."

"I'm planning to get a degree in law enforcement."

Direct, simple, self-explanatory. Good answer, young man. Test one passed. "That should be a good career path for you, Robert. I'll leave you for awhile to fill out this application. We'll talk more when you're finished."

I closed the door behind me and headed for the break room, while silently trying to calm myself. My new helper was a compact little powerhouse. I guessed him to be around 5'8" with well-developed chest and tapered flanks. Our shaking of hands brought to my attention his handsome forearm, as it sprang to life with well-defined muscles and hard-working tendons lightly covered with fresh sprouts of fur. Although still a teenager, his grip was firm and commanding. Heavy thighs completely filled the fabric of his jeans, which indicated he was an athlete of some sort, definitely lifted weights for his training. Of course, Robert to me was nothing more than eye candy, too young, just like all of them, end of discussion, end of thought process.

After finishing my break-room cigarette, I stepped into my office where Robert was signing his two-page application.

"Get it done ok?"

"Yes, sir. All spaces filled."

I quickly scanned the handwritten particulars on this youngster, zeroing in on the birth date. "So, you're 18. Senior year?"

"Yes. Eight months to go."

"On the wrestling squad, huh? How's the team looking?"

"I don't expect much. We only won 4 matches last year, but I won all of mine except for two."

"You play tennis, too. When does that start?"

"In March, but I'm not very good – just love to play."

"I still play every now and then."

He sat back with a look of curiosity. "Uh, no offense, Mr. Russell, but I can smell the smoke. Don't you get out of breath when you play tennis?"

I sat back myself and gave him a confident smirk. "Well, Robert, I can hold my own with about anyone who's come along so far."

"Oh, yeah? I bet I could run you ragged."

I liked his attitude. This little smart-aleck had me fired up in more ways than one. He had a charming expression of mischief on his face that begged me to take the bait, which I was willing to do. After all, with his age confirmed I no longer felt the need to remain close-minded about it. "Sounds like a challenge, Mr. Flynn. Want to try me?"

"Sure. Anytime you're ready."

"How about tomorrow?"

"When and where?"

Our arrangements for a social meeting fell nicely into place, all happening before the young man had even started working for me. I showed him around the warehouse and he helped me load a pretend order for a cart, and then we both took it to the designated department. Robert was sharp and quickly jumped in to handle the assignment while asking questions as they popped into his head. By five pm it was time for me to go home and I felt confident he could start working on Monday after school.

"You can be here by four?"

"Yes, sir."

"Ok, I'll schedule you to work weekdays from four until closing at nine pm. Meanwhile, I'll see you tomorrow at Scofield Park."

"Thanks, Mr. Russell." We again shook hands. "I'll pity you tomorrow."

"We shall see about that, Robert."

After he left, I returned to my office and looked again at the application. His previous summer's employment was with a residential roofing company; the summer before that he'd mowed lawns. These activities and the wrestling fully explained his shapely physique. My question was whether that fresh fur on his forearms was representative of the remainder of his body and I fully intended to find out.

Preliminary Exam

When I pulled into the parking lot by the tennis courts, Robert was waiting in his car. I parked next to him and he immediately jumped out to wait by my door.

"Hello, Robert. Are you pumped up for this?"

"Yes, sir, Mr. Russell."

"You can call me Matt here. No formalities necessary."

"Ok, Matt. Mind if I ask how old you are?"

"31 and I feel 18. You are about to receive the thrashing of a lifetime."

That playful grin of his returned. "Talk is cheap, Matt."

"Right you are. Here's a new can of balls. Let's volley for a bit."

"Hey, let me open those. I love the smell of new balls." He pulled the key and took a whiff of pressurized air escaping from the can. "Man, that's sweet."

I was amazed that he was making this so easy. We picked one of the three empty courts and unpacked our gear, then he handed me one ball, while he took two and headed for one of the baselines. Whereas I had dressed sharply in a navy blue warm-up suit, Robert wore gray sweat pants and zip-up sweat shirt with white t-shirt underneath. This being mid-October, the day was sunny but brisk with just a slight breeze.

The first tennis ball launched towards me hit the top of the net and fell to the court, but the next reached me and I soft-touched it back. As we casually volleyed back and forth, I could tell his forehand was respectable, but the backhand was not. His skill level was about half of mine, which was the perfect scenario. I could control the intensity of the action, while focusing on his every move.

"Well, Robert, I'm ready when you are. You can serve first when you're ready. Take as many warm-ups as you need."

I tossed the balls over the net so he had all three, then proceeded to strip off my warm-ups. He tried several times to fire a rocket, but hit the net each time. Finally, on the sixth try he got one over, in and was finished. "I'm ready. Let me get out of these sweats."

Soon, Robert was ready for action in navy blue gym shorts and the white t, arms and legs exposed. Part one of my mission was accomplished – legs matched the forearms.

"First set," Robert announced before serving his rocket attempt into the net. His second service was lobbed over and good. I knocked a medium velocity liner to his backhand, which he flubbed badly. This was the pattern, as Robert could usually keep the ball in play using his forehand, but anytime I needed to win a point all I had to do was target his other side.

I let him win on his service game, then slowly began to dominate him. As one game after another fell into my column, Robert's frustration grew, not with me, but himself. Soon he was cursing his name with each missed shot, increasing his anger all the way to the end of set one... Matt 6, Robert 1. We came together at the net.

"Man, I'm usually a little better than this," he admonished himself.

"Biggest problem I see is that t-shirt. It's too tight. How can you move in that thing?"

Now, the temperature at best was in the upper 50 degrees, but Robert wasted no time in removing that shirt to reveal what I had hoped to see. Healthy brown hair on his chest and a solid line trailing from his stomach to his gym shorts majestically enhanced his shapely muscles underneath. The shape of his torso was a perfect "V" and his belly slightly rippled. The chilled air caused his nipples to shrink into little knobs and the tips pointed forward from his well-developed pectorals. Part two of my endeavor was in the books.

We played two more sets and I was a bit more lenient with Robert, allowing him to win 2 games in set two and 3 in set three. With each switching of court sides after service, I thrust my hand towards his belly for the tennis ball exchange and my fake attack caused him to tense his muscles in defense. I liked that. This middle-section flexing game spurred me to quicken the tennis games for another side switch.

Robert was a gracious loser, "Well, Matt, you punished me pretty good. I think I've had enough for today."

"Next time I'll give you some pointers with your backhand. Your game will be a whole lot better after I get finished with you."

"Oh, good. I was afraid you wouldn't want to play against me again... not enough competition."

"Well, Mr. Wilson sent you to me for learning, so this can be part of it."

He put on his t-shirt, damn it, but was not ready to end our social togetherness. "I'm hungry, Matt. Wanna go get a hamburger or something?"

"Well, believe it or not, that's exactly what I was going to fix when I got home. Why don't you save your money and let me fry us up a few burgers? I live just a few blocks from here."

"Works for me. I'll follow you."

Lesson 1

"So, Robert, do you have a girlfriend?" The burgers sizzled, while I cut up the peripherals for toppings.

"Sure. We've been together about a year now."

"What's her name?"

"Theresa."

"Is it serious?"

"Maybe. We almost did it once, but I don't trust condoms, so I kept my jeans on and shot in my shorts."

I served the burgers and continued with this very interesting subject, as we talked with mouths full of ground beef patties and their surroundings. "Sounds like you respect her quite a bit. How about oral? Ever do that?"

"On her?"

"Or her on you, either way."

"No, we've never done that."

"Anybody ever suck your dick?"

He stopped chewing momentarily and turned red-faced, but shook his head and smiled with burger between his teeth. "Nope."

"Oh, man. You don't know what you're missing. When it's done right, there's nothing like it."

"That's what I've heard. Thinking about it's getting me excited right now."

I noticed that he was practically swallowing his food whole, seeming to be in a hurry for some reason. This poor, neglected man was so bright-eyed and eager to learn that he practically had paved his own path to this momentous occasion. From the moment we met, he'd followed my every step like a loyal puppy dog and now it was time for his reward, or at least time for me to find out if he would accept his reward.

Reaching under the table, I placed my hand on his belly and gave it a rub, "Well, now that you're a big senior it's time you find out about it. Mr. Wilson wants me to teach you and that's what I'm going to do. Finish your burger."

"I'll finish it later."

So much for my apprehensions, not that I had many to begin with. Apparently, Robert had none, as he followed me to the bedroom and asked for directions. "Should I get naked, teacher?"

"Please do."

I was more than impressed with the maturity of this young man, not only his open-minded attitude, but also his amazingly developed body.

For lesson one, I said nothing and touched nothing. Rather, I simply knelt between his thighs and took his semi-erect organ into my mouth and brought it to full strength. His release took awhile, as a small bit of uncertainty lingered in his mind, but eventually the years of pent-up curiosity came to fruition and the resulting volume of discharge reflected his suffering. I swallowed everything he had to give me, and then let go before I should have, done by design. That post-orgasm pain and pleasure punishment would be saved for another lesson.

Lesson 2

"Ok, Robert, now you know how it feels."

"It's the greatest feeling in the world, just like you said. Thanks, man."

"You're welcome, but not quite correct about the greatest in the world."

He sat up and swung his legs off the edge of the bed. "What do you mean?"

"The first time is never the best, because you're thinking about the event. Take a break and we'll have another lesson, which will be even better for you. The bathroom's right there if you need to go. I'll be right back."

I pointed off the bedroom and he headed in that direction, closing the door behind him. Meanwhile, I returned to the kitchen and gathered our plates and drinks. When Robert came out of the bathroom, I was waiting on the bed with the remnants of our lunch.

"Sit down and let's finish this. Don't want you losing your energy."

He climbed onto the bed and we both sat with our legs crossed Indian-style. Robert seemed completely at ease in my presence, even though he was naked and I wasn't. As we ate, I continued his tutoring. "Thing is, the best way to enjoy a blow job is to pretend like it's masturbation, except that somebody else is doing the work for you."

"Then what am I supposed to do?"

"Just kick back and fantasize about whatever turns you on."

"I'm not homosexual, Matt."

"I know that. Neither am I. I just like to suck dicks."

This caused him confusion. "What's the difference?

"Hey, there's a big difference between a little blow job and having someone put it in your ass. That's intercourse. This isn't."

"So, this is all you do?"

"That's it, nothing else. What you need to know is that this is the best way to tell how much a woman cares about you. If she's for real, she'll do this for you anytime. If she's truly devoted, she'll worship every inch of your body, not just your cock."

"You mean kissing me all over?"

"Oh, yeah. Kissing, licking, nibbling... the works. How's that for a fantasy?"

He moved the plate to one side, revealing a full-on boner. "Does that answer your question?"

Leaving the bed, Robert set his still-unfinished plate on a nearby dresser, and then returned to lay upon my mattress. "Show me, teacher."

This horny young man got his wish, as I set my plate next to his and began the lesson. "Now, in order to entice her, you've got to strike a pose of sacrifice. Give your body to her. Put your arms up past your head so they're out of the way, then let her go at it.

He stretched his arms out in a "V" towards the headboard.

"She'll probably start out by going for your mouth. She'll lay on top of you like this and lock lips with you."

I hovered over him but did not lay on top of him, nor did I go for the kiss.

"I ain't gonna lock lips, because I don't like it. She'll want her skin touching yours and that'll get both of you all excited."

"Hey wait," he interrupted. "Let me feel your skin against me, so I'll know what you're talking about."

This young fellow sure was eager to learn. I left the bed and stripped to my undershorts, and then resumed my position atop his prone body, chest to chest and with his exposed cock and my fabric-covered cock crushed between us. "Ok, after she buries her tongue down your throat for awhile, she'll slowly work her way towards her target." I put my lips onto his neck and gradually worked down to his chest with dry-lip kisses. "At this point, you should have your eyes closed and be thinking about whatever fantasy comes into your head. You've given yourself up to her, which is a way of showing how much you care for her. You totally trust her to work you over good while you drift off to another place."

This he did. With his eyes closed, Robert's body relaxed beneath me and I obediently worshiped him. No more words would be necessary.

My face was buried into his furry chest, as I kissed and occasionally wet-dotted his hairs with the tip of my tongue. Slowly, I worked my way to the left until my lips met his nipple. He tensed up slightly from this sensation but said nothing, so I lingered here for awhile. I circled the knob with a pointed tongue, then lightly scraped the top of the tip. As my touch intensified, Robert relaxed while his tit shrank. The tip rose higher into the air and my lips clamped hold, squeezing his pointed skin in my soft vise.

Robert arched his back ever so slightly, as this new sensation caused him to offer his beautiful knob up for further praise. Taking notes, I stored this point of interest for exploitation at another time. For now I needed to discover more of his hot spots.

Following the trail of hair, I dropped off the end of his sternum and worked on his sloping and tight stomach. My tongue lip was firmly pressed onto his skin, while lips occasionally pecked his hard abdominal surface. Each time he exhaled, Robert's stomach seemed to sink a little lower, as he sucked in his abdominal cavity to proudly exhibit its rock solid structure. He was shown my appreciation for his display. Working my way further down, my tongue and lips covered all of his stomach and lingered just above his stretched navel. To expose all of his belly, I raised up my torso an inch or two, grabbed his throbbing peter in my hand and bent it downward, tucking it under my chest. Lowering my weight onto him, I scrutinized his lower abdomen with my face inches above.

He collapsed and tensed his belly when my tongue made contact, just as he'd done when I'd shoved the tennis balls toward him. This only further highlighted the beautiful lines of muscle beneath his skin and I made my way for his navel. What a beautiful hole this was. Nicely oval and inset, a thin line of hair grew into it from the top and a thick one came out below. I delved into the depths with the tip of my tongue until making contact with that little knot of skin inside, which brought a slight moan from its owner. Robert slowly turned his head side to side with eyes closed, as he absorbed the pleasures of my navel attack. Working my tongue and lips inside and all around, those belly hairs were soon darkened with my spit while he flexed and undulated his hard abdominal muscles. Youthful masculinity lay inches beneath me. Robert's imprisoned cock pulsated under my chest.

I slid down a little further and took the tool into my hand. Guiding it to a vertical stance, I buried his dick into my mouth and lowered the boom. I took my lips straight down to press against his pelvic bone, my lips and nose tickled by his soft and curly pubic hairs. His penis was taken to the depths of my throat and I held it there, squeezing and crushing it between the tongue and roof of my mouth. I worked my throat muscles as though I was trying to swallow his sausage whole, contracting and massaging the sensitive head of his unit. Then I placed the palms of both hands onto his flattened belly and pressed down hard. The glorious mushroom pulsated inside me and I orally crushed his corona with all the strength I could apply.

With a mighty groan, Robert arched his back and fired a salvo of semen directly into my gut. That pumping pecker reverberated from its shaft base to its cock head, as one spurt after another shot out of his cannon. I kept my lips against his pubes the entire time, giving him that satisfied and manly feeling of deep penetration. Robert's spear was forced to impale the back of my mouth, while his body writhed, flexed and contorted, totally lost in the pure heaven of his orgasmic fantasy. Once I felt him start to come down a bit, I brought my lips up his pole and scraped my tongue against its hyper-sensitive underside. This caused him to let out another deep-toned groan of pleasure and one last contraction of come. I was finished with him, not yet ready to torture him with post-orgasmic sucking, so I licked dry his cock, transferred it to my hand and gently laid it onto his belly. Another easy comedown was granted.

The poor guy just laid there completely spent. His chest and belly were rising and falling at a rapid pace, as he slowly recovered from my lessons of worship. As for me, I stayed right there between his thighs, resting on my elbows and admiring my handiwork until Robert finally opened his eyes and raised is head.

"Holy shit. I can't believe how good that was."

"Told you so. Second one's always better."

I raised up to crawl off the bed and my loyal trainee soon followed. "Wanna know what I was thinking about, Matt?"

"No. You should keep that secret to yourself."

"How come?"

"If you ever want to use it again, you won't worry about me figuring it out. It would ruin things for you if you knew I knew."

"Yeah, that makes sense." He noticed that my penis was still fully engorged and pointing straight forward in its fabric prison. " Wow, you've got a big dick."

"Thanks. Looks like I'll have to fix myself later."

There was a long silence. I waited to see if Robert was interested in helping out with this, but he just smiled and looked to the floor. This was understandable and in no way was I disappointed. After all, I had far surpassed the activities planned for our first day together, but Robert, proving once again that he was just as clever as I'd suspected, came up with a plan of his own. He flung himself onto the bed and stretched his limbs into the same grooves that were still there from his recently-completed lesson. "Here, Matt. Can you jack off now?"

You better believe I could and did, reaching into a dresser drawer mid-stroke for a towel that one minute later was splotched with my creamy extraction.

"Finished?"

"Oh, yeah. Didn't you hear me?"

"Was that you grunting like a caveman?"

"That was me."

"I'm bushed."

"I'll bet. You want any more of your cold burger?"

"I probably ought to think about getting home."

"Ok. You think about it while I clean up our mess." Meaning our food mess, I picked up the plates and carried them to the kitchen where I filled the sink with soapy water and dumped everything in to soak. Back in the bedroom, Robert was asleep, his urge to go home superceded by his comfort with me.

There is no doubt that young Robert had decided to stay right there to get his dick sucked again and again and again. Make no mistake, I was tempted. Looking down at him nakedly sprawled on his back, so vulnerable, so at ease to be in my bed, I easily could have given him his desired marathon of blow jobs until he could take no more. I did not do that. Based on memories of myself when I was his age, I'm sure

Robert could have gone six or seven times, wearing me out before ever admitting that he'd had enough. For Robert and for me better things were waiting, but they could only come after he had been forced to live with his memories of my touch. I'd let him stew until next week, let him dredge up every fantasy buried in his brain, so that by the time our next tennis match was ended and he once again was in my bed, Robert would be hurting to give me the performance of a lifetime. For Robert, masturbation would never again fully satisfy him no matter how many times he jacked it during the week. He'd be back. I had no doubts.

After washing all of our dishes, I returned to find him still waiting, still dozing, and I awakened him with one final memory. Even I couldn't be in complete control all of the time. I sucked him off while he drifted in his state of semi-consciousness, midway between dream and reality, and once again Robert exploded with an impressive dose of his youthful seed. Two orgasms, three orgasms, when you're 18 what's the difference?

"Well, Robert, I think it's time for school to dismiss for this week."

"Yeah, probably should. Longest tennis match in history."

"Hmm... I guess you could always say if asked that we played a few sets, went to eat, and then played some more."

"And played and played."

Robert was unconcerned. My force-feeding him an alibi was unnecessary, for he had proven time and again that he was light-years ahead of other young men his age in the savvy department. For this reason, I took the risk of not telling him the importance of keeping our secret secret. There was little doubt that Robert liked what he had found and was planning to be protective of his discovery, properly selfish. This is one lesson in which Robert needed no instruction, and I had no intention of insulting him by saying it.

PART TWO - HEAVY LABOR

It pleased me no end to find that not only was Robert a good-looking and enthusiastic worker, but also a quickly-independent one. I'd scheduled myself to work from noon until 9 pm on Monday just so I could be there for him on his first shift, but it wasn't really necessary.

After we finished filling out the remainder of required forms for his hiring, I set him loose in the warehouse. He did everything required with minimal supervision or instruction, so after a couple of hours I cut him loose to work on his own while I spent most of the evening catching up on paperwork in my office. For the rest of the week, I worked my normal shift and only saw him for one hour, but on Wednesday he confirmed our next appointment.

"Tennis Saturday, right?"

"Sure. Same time and place, Robert."

"Ok, Mr. Russell, see you then."

On Thursday he reconfirmed and Friday re-reconfirmed. On Saturday he was waiting for me when I arrived, already on the court with shirt removed. Such a thoughtful opponent this Robert was. I showed him the correct way to use his backhand swing, standing behind him, taking his wrist in my hand and stroking it with him. We worked on the correct positioning of the feet and then I stood on the other side of the net to toss balls in his direction for practice swings. He remained totally focused on my instructions and made every effort to do it the correct way, so we volleyed for nearly an hour before I announced that he was ready to test that backhand in a real game situation. We played a couple of sets and he put his learning to good use.

Little by little, Robert gained confidence in his backhand, and subsequently his entire game. Scores: Matt 6-6, Robert 3-4.

"Looking a lot better."

"Yeah, I'm enjoying the game a lot more, too. Thanks, Matt."

"Next week we'll work on your service. Then you'll be the complete player. Each time you hit the courts you'll get better and better."

"That's what I want to be."

"Ready for some lunch at my place?"

He grabbed hold of his shorts and adjusted his hidden peter. "Yes, sir!"

After filling his belly with a big plate of spaghetti and sausage meatballs, I prepared him for today's lessons. "Well, Robert, let's get cleaned up. We've got a busy schedule ahead of us."

Lesson 3

What I meant was for each of us to shower, but Robert insisted that we clean the kitchen first and I certainly did not deny him this pleasure. While I finished drying what he had washed, Robert found all necessary items I'd left for him in my bathroom and washed himself for me. He came out of the bathroom with towel wrapped around his waist before proceeding directly to the bed. Removing the towel, he flopped onto the mattress refreshed and eager for more learning.

"Hang on there, partner. I need a shower myself."

I left him waiting and took a quickie. Upon my return, I found a naked Robert sprawled out spread eagle in the middle of my bed. One of the pillows was under the middle of his back.

"Lookee here, teacher. I've put myself on the altar of sacrifice."

"Ah, ha! So, I see the Amazon women have bound your wrists and ankles. Those ruthless savages. Your naked body is at their mercy. Soon, countless tongues will torment and taunt you, just to see how much one man can take."

Was this the fantasy he had entertained for the past seven days? Must have been close enough, because Robert reached to grab the corner posts of the headboard, stretching himself nice and tight. His cock lay on his belly, and what was half-way erect when I began my little speech was now fully charged and bouncing each time his heart beat. Standing at the end of the altar, I grabbed both of Robert's ankles and tightened him up a little more. Robert played his role well by letting out a slight moan, closing his eyes and preparing for his lesson.

"These evil bitches will stop at nothing to punish you."

I crawled onto the bed beside his chest. I assaulted him with friction warming hand rubs to his chest and belly. "These savages are ruthless. The entire tribe will have you. No part of you will be spared their cruelty." I leapt off the bed and knelt on the floor. Clutching an ankle in my hand, I laid a tongue to the sole of his right foot. He initially curled his toes in defense, peering over his chest to watch my assault, and then he arched back his toes to expose his foot to me. From the heel to the ball of his right foot my spit was painted onto his thick skin, while my right hand reached over to his left foot and manually massaged, wrapping my fingers over the top and rubbing a thumb up and down his manly arch. Lightly, I put my teeth onto the curve below his toes and gnawed the ball of the right foot.

Robert played right along with me, dropping his head to the mattress with another deep-toned groan of pretend pain and real pleasure. Soon, my tongue invaded the crevices between his toes, while the fingers of my right hand intermingled between the toes of his left foot. He bent back all ten toes and gave his feet to me, inviting this new found ecstasy. Then, without warning, I rudely ran my nails down the sole of his exposed left arch, which caused him to flinch and curl his toes forward. "These menacing females will torture you for hours. Their insatiable appetite to punish you knows no bounds." With a quick reversal of my position, I tongued his left foot while hand rubbing his right. Satisfied that Robert was well-acquainted with the pleasures of professional foot-worship, I moved to other parts.

"There is no limit to the cruelty of these savages." I climbed onto the bed and knelt beside his chest, as it was thrust upwards, stretched and vulnerable. "They unleash their fury in pairs. While those two work on your helpless feet, another two now brutalize your exposed chest. They show no mercy."

I encircled his right nipple with my lips and ruthlessly licked with my tongue. Simultaneously, his left nipple was taken between finger and thumb, then lightly pinched and twisted. Another groan of sheer pleasure rumbled from his gut and I saw him pull on the bed posts. His arms flexed and so did his chest, as he arched his back and thrust his tits higher, sacrificing them to my tantalizing torment.

In between my licking and sucking, I took him deeper into the fantasy. "These bitches have captured the ultimate male beast. It has been years since they have had such manly power in their presence. His incredible strength is now subdued. He belongs to them and they will do with him as they please."

"Oh, no. What are you maniacs doing to me?" Robert raised his head to witness the torture of his nipples. I had him where I wanted him, in the jungle, one powerful but defenseless man versus countless mouth-frothing females. He thrust forward his lower jaw and sneered with manly defiance. "You sadistic whores. You'll never defeat me." He strained his arms, expanded his chest, flattened his belly. "Do what you gotta do." He dropped his head, arched back his toes and thrust his hips into the air while clinching his scrotum, forcing his syrup-spitting cock to rise off his belly to stand midair.

This gap allowed me to maneuver my head under his penis and bury my face into his hard, stretched belly. I pressed my lips into him. I rubbed my face side to side into solid muscle covered in youthful hair. I licked those hairs to darkness, while guiding him deeper into his fantasy. "The evil Amazons unleash a full-blown assault. Their mouths show no mercy. They ravage your feet, belly, chest, tits, arm pits... twelve women versus one man... how much more can he take? No man has ever taken punishment like this... hour after hour... ungodly torture... with no escape... only your masculine strength can save you now."

Like an acrobat, I leapt over his thigh to kneel between both thighs. "No... not this... they wouldn't... they can't..." I put my tongue to his nuts, covering both with my lips.

"Oh, my god," Robert growled deeply. "Oh, you fucking bitch." His words were accented with breath, dramatized by masculine lust. "What are you doing to me?"

He spread his legs as far as they could go, opening his balls for me to munch. I wet-scraped with my tongue, dry-pinched with my lips, as Robert thrust his chest into the air, arching his back to a painful degree. He intensified his own pain to heighten his own pleasure, and with a sudden attack I simultaneously took his cock into my mouth, planted my left hand firmly into his belly and twisted the skin of his nuts with my right hand fingers and thumb.

Five frantic strokes from the base to the head of his cock did the trick. This tortured man was primed. Seven days of waiting followed by one hour of torment produced an explosion well worth the effort. His hands remained clasped to the head posts. His back arched higher than I thought possible. His manly groans echoed from wall to wall, as his tormented nuts contracted one mighty stream after another. With frantic stroking, slurping and swallowing, I desperately kept pace with him, a feat easier said than performed. His second and third spurts nearly matched the first for velocity and volume. I gave him no relief. My attack never altered in technique or speed, as I took from him his fourth, fifth and sixth eruptions, equal in velocity to the first three, but mercifully less in volume. Fucking he-man. Damned super-stud. That's what he was. That's what I'd made him.

And since his desired fantasy was to be subjected to bound torment, I chose this time to further punish him. Even though his body collapsed and his spurts faded to dribbles, I refused to stop stroking on him. Robert's magnificent penis was slow-stroked, his belly clawed by fingertips, his nuts mercilessly twisted and pinched. He convulsed. He twitched. He grunted, and he kept himself stretched to endure my aftershock assault upon his hyper-sensitive cock. His bulging corona was ruthlessly crushed, mercilessly scraped, and Robert contorted as though racked with bolts of electricity. He was racked, with bolts of pain and pleasure, with bolts of feverish, masculine lust, until he released his hands and raised up.

"Oh, god damn," he laughed, nearly in tears. "That's enough," he gleefully begged. "I... I can't take anymore."

He didn't have to. I transferred him to my hand and laid his cock onto his belly. Robert fell back across his pillow with his hands rubbing his chest. He was thoroughly exhausted, completely drained and wholly satisfied.

Leaving him alone on the bed to his own thoughts, I stepped into my bathroom, relieved my bladder, and returned with a hand towel to stand above him. He hadn't moved one inch. Nine or ten strokes later, a healthy dose of my semen saturated the towel and both men were happy.

"Man, you are too much." Robert rolled off of his pillow altar. "You about wore me out with that one."

"You're too young to be worn out."

"Don't know about that."

He headed for the bathroom to do what I'd done, and when he returned I had a suggestion for his rejuvenation.

"Feel better?"

"A little."

"Well, why don't you take another shower? That always recharges my batteries."

He took my advice, which worked. Robert came out clean and dry and fondling his peter, but I had a little surprise for him.

"Now that we're squeaky clean, it's time you work on another kind of stroking."

"Explain."

"Time for you to fuck."

Poor Robert was confused. "I thought you didn't do that."

"No, not me. Let me take you downtown."

"I don't understand. I know you're not going to fuck me, no way that's happening."

"No, no, ride with me downtown. We're going to pick out a hole for you to practice on."

"Male or female?"

"Whatever we can find."

A huge grin came over his face and with my help he quickly dressed himself. My help included one of my sweatshirts and one pair each of my clean underwear and socks. He completed his wardrobe with his own sweat bottoms and tennis shoes. Ready to cruise, we piled into my car.

Lesson 4

On a Saturday afternoon near the eastern fringes of skyscrapers, the sidewalks were lined with male hustlers congregated in the vicinity of Jackie's, the seediest gay bar in town. Nearby and south of here female prostitutes offered their services to passers-by, mostly around The Big Cohuna, a topless bar that featured erotic lap dances. This is where we started. I slowly drove the right hand lane allowing Robert to inspect the merchandise.

"Man, these chicks look rough," he observed.

Quietly, I giggled to myself, pleased that he reacted to the trashiest whores in town the way I had hoped. "Well, it's a rough life they lead. See any you like?"

"Not yet. Not even close."

I continued on, knowing full-well this crop of ladies would not suit him. "There might be some over on McGarrity, I'll try that."

"You might as well. This ain't working for me."

As we approached Jackie's on this two-lane, one-way street, all the youngsters were posing for us in their effort to make sure we knew they were available. I cruised at inspection pace, passing by all of them while scanning for one in particular, one who had expertly taken care of me on several occasions when I didn't feel like going through the stupid bar games, which was almost always.

At the end of the block, I spotted what looked to be my target leaning against a shelter for the city bus lines, so I pulled to the curb and shouted to him. "Hey, Jeremy!"

He stepped to the driver's door and leaned down with bright eyes of recognition. "Wow, where have you been?"

"Oh, here and there. Kinda busy. How's things?"

"Awful. Last jerk I had stiffed me. Kept me suckin' his nasty dick forever. Thought he'd never get off, then when he did he threatened to beat me up. Kicked me outta his car."

"Gotta use better judgement."

"Man, I'm hungry. Can you help me out?"

"Sure, hop in the back."

Jeremy had been to my house several times and I always took good care of him. He wasn't like most hustlers. He didn't do drugs and in a mysterious way seemed to keep himself clean and looking nice, comparatively speaking. Over the past year I had become a sort of lifeline for him, picking him up about once a month and letting him stay with me a day or two until his restlessness got on his nerves and mine.

I'd furnish him with Goodwill-purchased clothes always stored in my dresser drawer, plus I'd make sure he left with enough money to survive the streets for at least a few days.

He furnished me with world-class blow jobs anytime I was ready for one. I had gained his trust and he mine, but he wasn't really my type – average height but thin with long blond hair and blue eyes. His appearance was somewhat that of a flat-chested girl, which didn't work for me, but I was hoping it might work for Robert.

"Burger joint ok?"

"Sure, sounds great."

"Jeremy, this is my pal Jason."

Robert gave me a funny look before realizing I'd changed his name for the cover of anonymity. He turned to greet my friend in the back seat. "Hi, Jeremy, pleased to meet you."

"Likewise."

Here was one of the reasons I liked Jeremy. He didn't make any comments involving sexual innuendos or anything that would embarrass me, but rather he acted like a normal fellow, knowing that I would treat him with respect and his good conduct would be rewarded.

As for Robert, I wasn't getting a good read on how he felt about this situation, so I explained to him my relationship with Jeremy. Soon, I had them conversing about subjects of interest to teenagers, since Jeremy was only one year older than Robert. Everybody was comfortable by the time I pulled into the parking lot at Stanky's Burgers and Fries.

Robert and I sipped on chocolate malts and munched on onion rings, while Jeremy consumed an endless supply of hamburgers and french fries to make up for two days of nothing to eat. After he was satisfied, we headed back for the suburbs.

Jeremy stripped off his funky clothes in the garage so that I could put them and his unholy-smelling shoes in a garbage bag for disposal. After I told him what we planned to do and why *Jason* was there, he took a long, hot shower while Robert and I discussed upcoming events.

"You ever fucked this guy?" Robert was curious.

"No. I told you it ain't my thing."

"How do you know if he's any good?"

"He makes his living by it. He's got to be."

"Is he... you know, clean?"

"I keep him clean. We go to the clinic once a month so he can get checked. C'mon, Robert, you should trust me by now, I think. Believe me, I've trained Jeremy well. He knows what his job is and he knows to do it without saying anything stupid."

Robert's concerns dissolved. "You're right. I should trust you."

These were all legitimate questions, of course, but I needed for him to have no reservations in order for this to work for him. "It's ok, Robert. He's a good guy, just comes from a tough environment. It's all he knows so far, but I'm showing him the other side of things. He looks up to me, so when he's here he knows what I expect of him. You are in for a real treat, my friend."

That grin of enthusiasm finally returned. "Wow, my first fuck. I feel something growing down there."

"Yes, I see that. Let's get comfortable."

We both stripped. Robert sprawled onto the bed while I grabbed some baby oil and hand towels. Before I could acknowledge the healthy boner laying on Robert's belly, a clean and naked Jeremy entered the room to do it for me. "Holy shit."

Within seconds, Jeremy had the impressive tool buried into his mouth and Robert closed his eyes to enjoy this service.

"Don't get him off, just warm him up," I directed the proceedings, making myself comfortable by sitting on the mattress next to Robert with my back against the headboard. Something about Jeremy's long blond hair sweeping across Robert's beautiful belly caused my cock to rev itself up, which prompted Jeremy to leave Robert's to take mine. He slurped and stroked on my dick with his lips and tongue.

"Ok, Jason, time for you to move."

Robert left the bed while I positioned myself for the best view. Moving the pillows aside, I sat upright in the center of the mattress with my back still against the headboard and legs flat, spread wide. Jeremy positioned between my thighs, reinserted my dick to his mouth and started sucking away.

With Jeremy bent over and positioned between my legs, I connected the final piece of our puzzle. "He's all yours, Jason. There's the hole. Grab a towel and the baby oil."

He retrieved the oil, and then knelt onto the mattress near Jeremy's backside with his upper torso vertical.

"Grease up your dick, Jason."

"Ok. Like this?"

"Of course. Don't expect me to believe you don't know this part."

"You're right. Done this many times. Never used oil, though. Just lotion."

"Yuck."

Jeremy was oblivious to this conversation, wholly focused on satisfying my elongated tool. I stretched my arms side to side and clasped my hands on top of the headboard, then kicked back to watch the show. Pouring oil atop his cock with hand cupped underneath, Robert manually stroked his fully-engorged weapon before shifting forward on his knees to attempt entry.

"Lube up his ass with your fingers first. Leave the excess oil on him, so you can glide right in."

As Robert's slimy fingers rubbed the rim of Jeremy's anus, my hustler raised his butt cheeks higher, bringing his ass near the level of Robert's cock. He inched closer to his target, held his pole forward and guided the head to press against Jeremy's portal, and then pushed, and pushed, and grunted and pushed some more until he slipped past the barrier.

Jeremy stopped stroking on me and let out a small whimper, as Robert got a bit too excited a bit too fast.

"Slow down there, sparky. Let him get used to you being in there first. Just hang around the outer edge and work your way in further a little bit at a time."

Robert was quite pleased with himself, as was I. My view was perfect. I gazed over Jeremy's spine where Robert's upper half, one hand on his hip and the other cupping his balls and shaft, slowly poked forward with complete confidence. He gently moved his pelvis to loosen the inner rim of Jeremy's hole, gradually digging his way in deeper, while locking eyes with me. "Ooh, this is really tight," Robert/Jason exclaimed. "I like it."

"I think you're doing a fine job. Go ahead and explore – find your rhythm."

While Jeremy continued sucking on me, Robert increased his pace of thrusts. Soon, he clasped his hands onto Jeremy's hips and widened his stirring motions. Amazingly, Robert performed like a seasoned stallion, twisting and dipping his pelvis while plowing further into Jeremy's rectum. Then, sensing that his receiver was willing, Robert executed one manly thrust, grunted, and proudly acknowledged his achievement by raising both of his arms into a body-builder pose while flexing his chest. "Got it. All the way."

"Ok, Superman. Looking good."

"No, not Superman, Tarzan," and he pounded his chest while belting out the call of the jungle.

With such youthful enthusiasm exhibited before me, I nearly shot a wad right then and there, but managed to prolong my pleasure. I watched with delight as Robert clasped his hands behind his head and totally manhandled that quivering asshole in front of him. He'd twist, thrust forward, retract and come back for more, each time at different angles and with a gradually quicker pace. Each movement highlighted every muscle in his chest and belly, as he danced an erotic ballet of dominating intercourse.

I tried to hold out a little longer, but the sight of this incredible fuck master perfecting his newfound skills took me over the edge, so I whispered a warning. "Jeremy, I'm comin' at ya."

While I fired my load, Robert grabbed hold of Jeremy's hips and drove his cock home with ram-rod precision and power. Pounding the receiver's butt cheeks into tenderized meat, he rapidly thrust his mighty organ into the depths, retracting an inch and then returning for maximum penetration. With a deep-toned and animalistic grunt, he sprayed Jeremy's innards with heavenly come, while continuing to frantically stroke in and out.

Jeremy drained me, seemingly oblivious to Robert's pounding him from behind. He relentlessly drove that spear into his target, repeatedly and rapidly firing away with pile-driving efficiency, until the intensity on his face began to lessen. Despite this, Robert's dominating thrusts continued even though I doubt he had much left to shoot.

It was as though he didn't want to let go of the moment and neither I nor Jeremy seemed to mind. He stroked his cock into and out of the deepest part of Jeremy's hole, while grunting and gasping for air. His intentions were obvious. Robert wanted a doubler, a back to back, second orgasm. This re-energized my cock like crazy, so I placed my hand on Jeremy's head to keep him on me, which I hoped would motivate my student to success. However, not all could be so bliss. Robert had an accident. In his uncontrolled desire to continue fucking, he pulled back too far and his cock slipped out, at which time he frantically tried to reinsert.

"Oh, no, damn it."

"What's wrong?" I played stupid. "You shot it all, didn't you?"

"I... I don't know." He desperately tried to get back inside, but panic caused his hard-on to fade, making it more and more difficult for him to regain entry. "Damn it to hell, I'm losing it."

"It's no big deal, Jason. Save some for later."

"No, I screwed it up. After all that, I screwed it up."

Poor guy. Defeated, he moved back with a look of disappointment, as though he had failed me, or failed himself. Either way, I tried to console him. "Looked to me like an old pro in action. Jeremy, what do you think? Did he screw it up?"

"No friggin' way, man. You felt great, Jason. I dunno what you're talking about."

We got Robert laying down in the middle of the bed and flanked him, Jeremy to his left and me to his right. I cleaned off his peter with one of the towels, while we both continued to pump his ego. Our hands stroked and massaged on his chest and belly, which caused him to put his arms up and tuck his hands behind his head, but still he was clearly frustrated. "Can't believe that happened."

I showered him with a motivational speech. "What happened, Tarzan? You fucked and fired your weapon... that's what it looked like to me, like you wrote the book on it. You were going at it like some kind of wild animal."

Jeremy added his accolades. "Yeah, Jason. Wish I could have seen it, too."

"Sure, I thought I was watching a fuckin' porn star, you hot dog."

Soon, we had him smiling again and fully satisfied with himself, while Jeremy and I thoroughly enjoyed making the little man feel like a big one. I don't know about Jeremy, but I meant every word of it.

Suddenly, it was time for Jeremy to leave. "Be right back."

Robert looked up. "Where's he going?"

"We're about to find out just how bad you screwed it up, as you say."

On the other side of the bathroom door, rumbles of liquid farts echoed from the toilet bowl, which told me Robert had passed the test.

"What goes in must come out. That's your come you hear exploding in there."

"Oh, man that's too much," Robert cracked up laughing. "I never thought about that part of it."

When Jeremy returned, he was wearing a big smile. "No, Jason. I'd say you shot plenty and I got all of it. You wanna see?"

"God, no.," I interjected. "Get in there and flush that... please."

With Robert's discharge in the whirlpool, Jeremy rejoined me on the bed to worship our hero. He laid on his back in the center of the mattress, no pillows, hands folded under his head. Our fingers and palms soothed every part of him and I verbally elevated him to the elite list of prized students. "You are really something. Did you notice I never said a word after you got started? Hell, there was nothing to say. Power, grace, you've got it all. Just a non-stop fuck machine, that's what you are."

Robert looked up at me, turned his head towards Jeremy, and then closed his eyes to bask in our praise. His ego was pumped, his chest and belly lovingly massaged. His face was relaxed, beaming with pride by way of satisfied smile. Robert's comfortable acceptance of our hero worship reminded me of a little boy triumphantly showing off his new bicycle the day after Christmas. Robert's newfound toy was situated between his legs and we had it doing things he never dreamed it could.

By the time we finished with him, Robert knew damned good and well that he alone was the star of this show. After all, that's what I wanted him to be.

Lesson 5

With our endless attention lavished upon him, Robert's peter had swollen to full force, ready for action. There was nothing more need be said, so I shut my mouth from speaking and used it for licking. Jeremy joined in and we saturated Robert's muscular torso with our spit. For a good thirty minutes, Robert enjoyed the warm wetness of our tongues upon his chest, stomach, legs, feet, arms and hands, until he was thoroughly primed and physically begging for us to touch the most important parts. I did that after indicating to Jeremy what he should be doing. While I munched on Robert's regenerated balls and teasingly licked his slime-spitting cock, Jeremy re-lubricated his own ass and prepared to mount our young steed. Robert? He did nothing other than to lay flat with eyes closed and feel. Jeremy was ready, so I addressed our super stud. "Time for you to fuck up. Any woman worth her salt will enjoy riding up and down on this pole of yours. If she doesn't, there's something wrong with her."

As I suspected he might, Robert reached for the bed posts and latched on. He stretched himself, surrendered to losing himself in whatever fantasy he desired.

This lesson would be Jeremy in control. His pace would determine when Robert could bust his nuts, a complete reversal of the previous lesson.

With knees straddling Robert's hips, Jeremy lifted himself to the top of the pole, positioned it to the rim of his anus and slowly glided back down with Robert inside him. Jeremy sat right down onto Robert's pelvic bone, straining his muscular innards to crush Robert's cock in his warm vise.

Fully confident in Jeremy's abilities, I resumed my own attack of tongue and lips, maneuvering around Jeremy to saturate the hairs of Robert's muscular thigh. Starting with his left leg, I drifted onto his knee cap, then his calf and then his ankle. Before attacking his left foot, I encircled his ankle with my fingers, stretching his leg on a simulated rack. Robert's foot was saturated with spit, Robert assisting by arching back his toes to open up his arch, while Jeremy mesmerized Robert's cock with torturously lingering glides up and down, each round trip consuming nearly sixty seconds. My round trip took me off the bed, kneeling on the floor to work on Robert's right foot. His response was the same, as he exposed his strong arch for me to lick.

His right leg was stretched as I crawled onto the bed. His calf and the fur adorning it were made slick with saliva, as was his knee cap and his thigh. Lower extremities serviced, I moved around Jeremy and knelt beside Robert's chest. He opened his eyes and smiled at me before attempting to participate by raising his hips to thrust his cock in unison with Jeremy's anal strokes. He may have thought this is what I wanted, or perhaps he wanted this himself, but either way his behavior was unacceptable.

"No, Tarzan, I don't think so." My fist pressing onto his belly forced him to the mattress, while emphasizing my wishes. "The tribe has bound you to this pedestal for a reason. This is their breeding hut."

Jeremy slowly rode the pole, as I put my tongue to Robert's right nipple, the one nearer me. Instantly, he strained his arms, posturing in bondage mode. With the fist of my right hand firmly pressing his belly, the finger and thumb of my left hand lightly pinching his tit, I told the sad tale of Tarzan's plight.

"They fear the power of the amazing white man, so they have made him their prisoner. They must have his seed. They will infuse its incredible power into their tribe. The mighty Tarzan will be milked until all are satisfied."

Pressing down a bit harder to his belly with my fist, I directed the taunting to him. "Yes, Tarzan. They will crush the come out of you again and again. All in the tribe will feel your power. They will ravage your helpless body with tongues and lips. You will surrender your masculine seed to them."

Robert raised his head with a groan. He watched me twisting his tit, looked at my fist grinding into his belly atop his navel. He grunted, ape-like, Tarzan-like. With a long gaze towards Jeremy and another grunt, Robert dropped his head to mattress and drifted into his jungle of torment.

Jeremy quickened his pace, but I motioned for him to linger, and so he sat on Tarzan's pelvis and squeezed the throbbing cock in his rectal grip. Taking his cue from my pointing to Tarzan's chest, Jeremy leaned forward and delicately clamped both of our prisoner's nipples between fingers and thumbs. As for me, I maneuvered beneath Jeremy to bury my face into Tarzan's hard, flattened hair-covered middle section.

With the nipples manipulated, belly and penis crushed, Tarzan flexed his mighty muscles. He strained against the bedposts to further stretch himself, then expanded his chest while sucking in and tightening his belly muscles. The power beneath my lips was incredible. I pressed my face deep into his solid wall of muscle, and then raised myself enough to lick and kiss.

Jeremy's flexing innards crushed the cock inside him. His twisting fingers and thumbs stimulated sensitive tits, while my tongue and lips saturated every inch of the stomach, belly and navel. As if this wasn't enough torment, I added verbal taunts in between my licking.

"There is no mercy for Tarzan. He fires his come into one savage, only to find himself mounted by another. No rest... no rewards, only the endless extraction of his powerful sperm. No other man could possibly stand up to such punishment... none but the mighty lord of the jungle himself."

Animalistic groans and grunts were the only sounds coming from our victim. With eyes closed and lower jaw forward, he continued to strain against his bindings, as his incredible body was ruthlessly attacked. Jeremy took my cue and released Tarzan's nipples. He sat upright on the impaling penis and slowly raised his buttocks, inches at a time. Once he reached the top of the throbbing pole, he agonizingly began a lingering descent. My belly assault never ceased, and with my left hand I rubbed Tarzan's chest taking great care to scrape my thumb and fingertips across his shrunken and protruding tits.

Poor Tarzan was taken to the brink of ecstatic madness. He arched his back and strained his arms to further simulate his stretching. He moaned with pleasure. He grunted with defiance, and as Jeremy gradually quickened the pace of his rise and fall, crushing the diameter of our victim's cock to nothingness, I reached behind him with my right hand and put it to Tarzan's swollen nuts. I rubbed them. I delicately scratched them and I twisted and pinched them. On his self-imposed rack, Tarzan struggled with a merciless assault upon his chest, tits, belly, penis and nuts until he suffered no more.

All breathing stopped. Every muscle flexed to capacity. Tarzan shot his load.

Bouncing and crushing like a maniac, Jeremy rode up and down Tarzan's impaling spear. My belly licking and chest and tit rubbing, along with my nut twisting and nut pinching, tortured Tarzan into unholy orgasm. As his incredible tool contracted again and again to jettison his seed, Robert violently thrust his hips upwards, forcing Jeremy and me to rise with him. We did not alter our pattern of attack. We continued at a frantic pace, as Robert arched his body, sacrificing himself in an incredible display of masculine strength and stamina. He held his position throughout the ordeal, his powerful spine and legs keeping all three of us aloft, until he slowly returned from jungle to bedroom, the bounty from his nuts wholly extracted. Only then did his bridge collapse. He once again laid flat with hands still grasping the bedposts, with Jeremy and me still assaulting him as though nothing had changed. And again, Robert's body twitched and contorted from the torture of his spent cock.

Robert's head turned side to side with eyes closed, while Jeremy sat on him, still crushing him, and I mercifully released his emptied nuts. Now, I kissed rather than crushed Robert's middle section. It was for my pleasure more than his, as I inhaled its hard, raw beauty, its surface rapidly rising and falling, expanding and sinking to replenish muscle with oxygen.

There are events that demand silence. This was one. Only with silence could we cling to what we felt, perhaps extend the intensity for a few minutes more. Our untangling of bodies, wiping of oil and semen, all was done in silence, leaving us once again with our exhausted hero in the middle and his head comfortably supported by two pillows. We flanked him, Jeremy and I.

Jeremy slept curled up on one side, his head on Robert's chest; I slept on the other, my head on Robert's belly. I don't know how long we slumbered in comforting recuperation, but I do remember that Robert was the first to speak.

"Hey fellas, I gotta piss."

Fair enough. We helped him from the bed because his spine had stiffened, and then we listened as he let go a seemingly endless stream. The bedside clock told Robert it was 9:58. "I think I better go home. My parents will wonder what kind of tennis match goes on for ten hours."

Jeremy just looked at me with disappointment, but I knew better than to push our luck. "Ok, Jason. We had one helluva time."

"Yeah, me too. It was great meeting you, Jeremy."

"Same here. See ya."

We watched him dress in his original clothes, leaving mine on the floor where they had been all evening. I slipped on my underwear to escort him from the bedroom and to the door.

"Matt, I guess I'll see you Monday."

"Sounds good, Robert. See you then."

Surprisingly, he leaned towards me and pecked my cheek with a kiss. "I really appreciate everything you've shown me."

"You're becoming quite the manimal."

"Yeah, whoever marries me sure will be surprised on our honeymoon."

"Darn right. She'll know she made a good choice."

Fantasies of Robert prompted me to shoot healthy doses of come into the mouth of Jeremy. This occurred numerous times for the remainder of the weekend until he was ready to go back to Jackie's. I dropped him off Monday morning wearing a clean set of clothes and carrying a sufficient supply of cash, which he kept inside his sock and underfoot. Makes you wonder where some of those greenbacks in your pocket might have been before you got hold of them, but let's not think about it too much.

PART THREE – ANOTHER HUSTLER
(THANK YOU MR. FLYNT)

The next Saturday began just as the previous. Robert was waiting for me with shirt removed. We worked on his service, and then he got a refresher course on the backhand and we were ready to play, resulting in scores of Matt 6-4, Robert 3-6. Yes, that is correct, Robert legitimately won a set from me and was elated. So was I. His first reward was a high protein lunch of steamed chicken breasts, pasta and peppers. Next came a mutual shower, which he suggested we execute in order to save me water, the thoughtful soul. After we marched naked into my bedroom it was time for his most important lesson to date.

Lesson 6

"So, teacher, are we going downtown to look for Jeremy?"

"Nah, I think your fucking skills are more than adequate. What you need to know is how to give that woman of yours a blow job."

This stumped him good. "Huh?"

"Eating pussy, boy! You've got to know how to do it right."

"Ah, hell, that's no big deal. You just open it up and start licking. Right?"

"Wrong. You've got to find her little peter, then she'll squirm like she's being electrocuted. She'll love you for life."

The poor guy was totally confused now. "What the hell are you talking about? Her little peter? Women don't have dicks."

"Oh, yes they do. Similar to ours, but in miniature. Look here."

I opened up a desk drawer to retrieve one of my prized possessions – a 15 year old *Hustler Magazine*. Turning the pages, I found the article of interest. One of my heroes, Larry Flynt, had put together a pictorial of vaginal closeups, complete with descriptions and diagrams showing that little peter as clear as could be. Using her fingers to spread open the vulva, that woman's clit appeared to be right there inches away from our tongues. I pointed to it.

"See that right there? That's the clitoris and the hood that covers it."

"Hey, it does kinda look like a tiny dick."

"Sure does and when you touch it, she gets the same sensation as when someone touches your dick right there." I reached down and rubbed my finger underneath his mushroom, which was already filling with blood. "That's what a lot of men don't understand. They waste their time licking the vulva. That's the part you see hanging out all around here." Pointing to the soft tissue just inside the pubic hair, I diagramed the buffer zone. "The vulva is sensitive, but the clitoris is hyper-sensitive and until you reach it she ain't gonna get off. She'll be disappointed in both the event and you. You can warm her up out here, but right in there is your target and when you hit it, you've got to know how to use your tongue. Master this and she'll worship the ground you walk on."

He took the magazine from me and sat on the bed, thoughtfully studying the series of pictures. Robert first looked curious, then a bit intimidated. "You ever been in there?"

"Oh, sure, when I was about your age."

"You learn it from this?"

"Yep."

"What did it smell like?"

"Not bad. Can't describe it, really."

"What did it taste like?"

"About the same as a dick. Just skin. If it's clean and fresh, there's no problem. The first one I did was clean and I rather enjoyed it, but only because she went crazy when I touched it, just like Larry said she would. I'm telling you, I thought she was gonna jump up through the roof of my car, but then she relaxed and let me get her off. Problem is, it's hard to work on that little thing. It's more like licking on the nipple of a baby bottle, but you talk about reaction, I think she wanted to marry me right then and there."

"You ever do a smelly one?"

"Yeah, the next one I did tasted and smelled like warm shrimp... almost rotten. After that, I decided it wasn't my bag. By that time, I pretty much had figured out that I prefer sucking on a man's penis. More to work with, plus they don't get all slimy and nasty tasting. If they do, you can just wash them off with a wet cloth, then get back to work."

"God, I think I'd puke if it smelled in there. How do you even get your tongue in that deep?"

"Look, it's not the same as how I suck on you."

I sat on the bed with my back against the headboard and legs spread flat on the mattress. "Give me the magazine."

He handed it over and sat next to me, as I pointed to the picture. "See, when you get in there, you've got to use your tongue to lift back the hood, kind of like the foreskin on a man's dick if he isn't circumcised. Once the full clit is exposed, you get your lips in there, then use your tongue to massage up and down the length of it. Believe me, after you start doing that, it won't take her long to finish."

Robert looked me in the eye, then glanced down to see my penis had shriveled to near nothingness, the result of that oversized vagina staring me in the face. Looking again at the picture of the woman's little peter, then back to me, he gave me a half-hearted grin. "Looks kinda like your dick looks right now."

"Aw, It ain't that tiny. Is it?"

"Nah, I's just razzin' you."

"Well, now you know why I'm this way. That woman's organs right there turn me cold. I notice it seems to make yours go the other direction."

His cock was rock solid and waiting for attention, but Robert ignored my lead in and took us another direction. "You want me to practice on you, don't ya?"

"Ah, well geez, uh," I couldn't think of any reason to stop him. "If you want to try. I guess as long as I'm looking at this magazine, I should be able to keep it mushy for you."

"I hope you don't." Robert slid down the mattress and knelt between my thighs. He took a chunk of skin between finger and thumb, then lifted my tiny peter up and away from my balls. I closed the magazine, laying it aside so I could watch my precious student lower his head and open his mouth. He was determined to give me this pleasure and I was willing to let him go for it.

Dry lips touched the head of my cock, then worked down just past the rim. Next, he tried his tongue. Robert remembered everything I had done to him, as he wet the underside of my mushroom and began to lick it. Cautiously, he took the still-flaccid meat a little further into his mouth, all the while lightly using his tongue to moisten my helmet. The event – not necessarily the sensation – forced my cock to fill with blood. Within seconds, what used to be my little peter became a full-blown weapon. All of the patience I had shown, all of my careful preparation and steady, authoritative instruction had come to fruition. Robert Flynn, this virile, muscular and incredibly handsome young man, was sucking my cock.

Gaining confidence, he lowered his lips further down my shaft while continuing to delicately lick underneath it, but as my length and width grew even stronger, Robert's enthusiasm turned to apprehension. His tongue no longer participated, as each time he tried to lick me his gag mechanism would kick in. He'd back away, recover, then try again, only to be greeted by a more violent convulsion.

Because of his struggles, my erection began to fade and I knew he was finished with this.

"Robert, it's ok. You got the gist of it."

He removed my dick from his mouth. "I thought I could get you off, but I'm about to throw up."

"It's not your thing, don't worry about it."

His once raging hard-on now was deflated to match mine. Both of our dicks looked like they wanted to crawl into a corner and die so I motioned for him to lay beside me, and although he seemed disappointed I could tell he was relieved that his ordeal was over.

"Sorry, Matt."

"I don't need you to get me off, Robert. I just need you to be yourself and be here with me. That's what gets me off."

As I reached over to stroke his chest, he turned, kissed my cheek and granted me a most precious gift. "I'm staying here tonight. I've already told my parents that I'm sleeping over with a wrestling pal of mine they know."

My penis surged upwards like a rocket. "Tell you what, Robert, I guarantee you won't regret it."

Lesson 7

The final bit of knowledge I wanted to pass on to him was this: you scratch my back and I will take you to utopia. I did not need to tell him, because he soon enough would know how much I appreciated his attempt to please me.

My look persuaded him to take his position spread eagle on the mattress and receive what I call the works. This is a prolonged session of intense body worship, using my tongue, lips, hands and fingers to fondle every crevice, every follicle of hair and every inch of skin that can be reached.

After 30 minutes of this, the male organ is beyond being fully charged. More than likely it is ready to explode. This is the environment to where Robert was taken, which meant it was time for the ultimate works, techniques used on him that were beyond his wildest imagination, and this time, I had nothing to tell him. His mind was free to go wherever it pleased.

His neglected penis was finally taken by my mouth and held halfway inside for the longest time with no hint of a finishing touch. Instead, it was put through a four-phase punishment. First, the judo chop. The outside of my right hand was placed to the left side and onto the base of his cock, while the outside of my left hand did the same midway up the shaft on the right side of his organ. Then, my hands came together, squeezing and bending his hardened pole, while my wet lips surrounded the head and my tongue brutally scraped under his mushroom.

The ecstatic torment continued for untold seconds, until I removed my hands and switched their positions to bend him the other direction while again stroking him with oral precision. Robert lay quietly with eyes closed, his mind lost in a far away fantasy land. Feeling he had endured this long enough, I released my hands and allowed his forceful penis to straighten itself.

With my lips still wrapped around him just past the rim of his helmet, I executed punishment number two – the punch. Forming fists with both hands, I pressed my knuckles onto either side of his shaft base, then resumed sucking on him like the nipple of a baby bottle. As the vise tightened at the bottom of his pole, my mouth took the head of his cock and bent it to the left, then the right, while my lips and tongue sucked and slurped. The pattern was repeated over and over, until I sensed an eruption coming and quickly removed my knuckles to leave his pulsating tool wondering, unfulfilled, and held motionless in my warm but unstimulating mouth.

I waited for everything to calm a bit before beginning punishment number three – the fold. Removing his dick from my mouth, I held it steady with a finger and thumb cock ring at its base. The next move was to shift myself over his thigh to kneel beside his left hip. Taking the thumb from my right hand, I placed it onto the triangle of skin under his mushroom, while wrapping my index finger across the top of his helmet. With a firm squeeze, I bent his cock towards his belly until it was shaped like the letter L. The sides of his shaft flared outward and my lips clamped onto the fold. I tightened and lessened the pressure with my lips on his shaft, while pumping the still-moistened head between my finger and thumb. The tongue also was involved, as it licked and scraped the middle of his shaft in conjunction with my squeezing lips. Then, in a further display of pleasurable cruelty, I reversed grip, shifting my right hand to the base and left to the head. His cock was now bent the other direction towards his feet and the gnawing of lips and licking of tongue was repeated on the top side of his tormented organ.

Punishment number four would finish him. I again positioned myself to kneel between his thighs in preparation for the nut crusher. No hands here, only mouth. Very simple, his cock was swallowed whole, my lips pressing into his pubes and his dick standing vertically in wet darkness. Slowly, my lips moved towards his corona, my tongue scraping with every inch traversed until only the top-half of his cock was covered. From vertical to horizontal, his penis was brought down atop his nuts, still in my mouth and pointing to the foot of the bed. My lips stayed midway on his shaft. My tongue and roof of mouth sucked him like a giant straw. My fingertips gently massaged his compressed nuts. The thickness of his shaft stretched the sensitive skin of his ball sac, as the orbs inside split down the middle, flaring out on either side of his cock.

Robert did not allow me to continue this punishment for long, however, because his come soon flooded my mouth. His 60 minute ordeal produced the desired result – an intensely satisfying orgasm to please both giver and receiver.

The study course had ended. Never again would we be student and teacher, but playtime companions, bedtime partners, or if you wish to stretch the imagination, lovers. His announcement to me that he would be staying the night only further solidified our mutual admiration, plus it convinced me that he should be rewarded in a most significant way. Leaving the bed, I retrieved my baby oil and set it on the bedside table. We laid together and snoozed for awhile, as I allowed him to recuperate from "the works."

After 30 minutes or so, I made sure we were in a spoon position with my back nestled against his chest. Reaching behind me, I wrapped my fingers around his penis and squeezed it, fifteen seconds being the time needed for my youthful wonder to sport a full erection. From that point forward, Robert took charge of the action.

He turned me onto my belly, smothering me with his masculine fur and muscle before professionally entering my ass. Robert's performance was not the dramatic display of animalistic dominance he had shown the week before, but one of a caressing, loving man, one who respected and cared for me as much as I did him. We connected in more ways than one, a connection that would seal our friendship for years to come.

In a mere four weeks I had transformed him from a sexually fearful and naive youngster to a masterful stud, fully charged and always ready for sex. That entire weekend, any time we had reason to leave the bed, Robert would proudly strut from bedroom to bathroom to kitchen and back with his chest puffed up and dick swaggering, fully confident in himself and his libido.

Of course, little time was spent anywhere besides the bed, and since he had proven to me that having a dick in my ass wasn't such a bad thing, provided it was *his* dick, he was not only allowed but persuaded to further tenderize me to his heart's content. In this lesson Robert was the teacher, I the student, as he showed me my favorite position for accepting his masterful fuck tool, done so we could face one another.

He hooked the back of my knees with his elbows and raised my legs, draping them over his shoulders. Once his hands were free from assisting his cock with entry, he reached back to grab hold my ankles, lifting and spreading my legs to the shape of a V. And framed between this V was Robert's V, his chest, his belly, protruding forward in a glorious display of hard-working and stretched muscle. His fur was there for me to touch, his chest for me to rub, his tits for me to tweak, his belly for me to massage, his navel for me to poke and his arm pit hairs for me to tug. Most of all, I could see him. I could watch his flexing, undulating muscles dominate me with his masculine power, further emphasized by his cock, his impaling and overwhelmingly glorious, manly cock, as he stimulated my bowels with masterful thrusts in and out from up and down and left and right. Robert filled me up in so many ways. He feminized me, for in the presence of such a man there can be but one dominant partner, and Robert's incredible masculinity made me wonder what I'd ever done to deserve such a treasure as this.

I lost count of how many times he got off during our first overnighter, whether it be in my mouth or my ass, but Robert remembered. He announced it before leaving early Sunday evening.

"Man, I shot it nine times. I should be worn out, but I ain't."

"You've set a high standard. Hope you can live up to it."

"Don't worry," he dry kissed me on the lips. "Won't be a problem at all."

The weekend was such a success that it paved the way for our future. He continued to work at the department store warehouse until graduation, while the Saturday tennis lessons were a weekly event into winter and beyond. We moved it inside by my joining a club with indoor courts, and then proceeded with our regular bedroom follow-ups. In the spring his newfound tennis skills took him to the state regional finals before he suffered his first defeat.

He returned to his roofing job in the summer after announcing to his parents that he was moving in with me. Our weekends became a nightly affair. We no longer had a need for Jeremy, but we still occasionally dragged him off the streets for some three-way action to spice things up a bit. Robert was the one who eventually convinced Jeremy to retire from hustling. With an enthusiastic attitude, he secured employment with a big discount store, then began climbing up the ladder from stock boy to department manager and soon had his own apartment, his own car and his own man-friend.

The next fall, Robert began studying at a local college for a degree in criminology. He graduated and applied to the police academy. In both instances, he ranked near the top of his class.

It was nearly two years after this that he finally settled down into the married life and got to dazzle that female I had trained him for. She obviously loved him enough to wait until he was ready to make the move and I'm sure she was glad she did, but despite all of this Robert never forgot about me. Even though they now have kids, he still calls me from time to time and makes arrangements to visit my bedroom, where I welcome him with open everything.

He says nobody will ever treat his dick the way I can do it and I've never argued with him on that point. I'm never disappointed in anything he does or has done, because I fully understand his desires. Like all of us, a man's situation dictates what he must do. Ambitions and requirements change. Co-workers ask about your wife; parents ask for grandchildren; we all go through cycles of upheaval and it is useless to fight these needs.

Robert has given me 11 of the best years anybody could ever hope to have. When we lived together, everything he did pleased me like no other person could, and even though those moments are now further apart in time, nothing will ever change what we are to ourselves and to each other. I trained him well.

RAIL YARD TRILOGY

PART ONE - FLEETWOOD

When I worked for the railroad, my job was to off-load vehicles from the auto racks (railcars filled with new automobiles) brought into our fenced yard (the ramp). That was my day job. On weekend nights, I would patrol the ramp to watch all the automobiles parked there in waiting for distribution by trucks to all parts of the immediate area. Mine was a security function, paid for by the automobile companies to the railroad so that at least one human being would be on that lot 24 hours a day to guard their property. My weapon? A wireless radio. With this I communicated to the nearest dispatch tower any unusual activity or breach of the fence surrounding our ramp.

I was there 11pm to 7am Friday through Monday, at which time I'd begin my new week for the full-time day job. During this security watch I usually had little to do. The exception was when the railroad guys would bring the "spot", which was a string of auto racks filled with brand new automobiles. Most nights, this would be done before I arrived, but sometimes they were late and I would help them set the racks up at the proper spacing, so the day guys like me could connect them with heavy steel plates to drive the cars off the racks, down the ramp and onto the lot.

A yard engine was used to bring the racks in to the ramp and set them up, then the crew chief would join me on the ground to communicate by radio to the engineer in the cab of the locomotive, telling him to shove or pull the racks, based on what I said, based on my measuring stick. It was wood, about four feet long, and because I carried it with me when setting the spot, I was called the stick man.

But not George. He called me Kenny. George was the crew chief on the late shift always assigned to bring in the spot if the previous crew hadn't gotten around to it. He was a thick, burly man with meaty and hairy forearms. Laid back and easy-going, George always took time to talk to me about the happenings in the main yard and the company itself. For whatever reason, he always seemed to be down in the dumps and I never could figure out why. Whether he was unhappy with the job or something else I never knew, but I would always try to lighten his spirits best I could.

"What's going on tonight, George?"

"Same ol', same ol', Kenny. Looks like the Frisco will soon be history."

"So the merger was approved?"

"Yeah, right. Merger."

Those were the days when bigger railroads were starting to take over the smaller ones. Although they were called mergers, they really were buyouts. The end result is what you see today – only four major railroads remain in the United States, not counting the few regionals that have sprung up.

We were fortunate to work for one of the big ones, but every time a merger took place, all the guys would get bumped down the seniority ladder from new guys coming in from the defunct railroad. Union rules dictated this.

"So how far is that gonna set you back this time, George?"

"Don't know for sure, but probably about 20 men."

"Well, at least you know your pension is intact."

He smiled a bit. "Yeah, that's true, but it sure gets frustrating. Pisses my wife off every time this happens. She was expecting me to get a raise in two months, but I doubt if she'll get it now."

"Is she givin' you hell about it?"

"24 hours a day. Work my ass off and she's never satisfied. Never enough."

Poor guy. Domestic strife really turns me on, so I queried a little further. "Don't you get any thank you's or displays of affection?" I tapped him on the bicep with a fist, flashing a mischievous grin.

"Few and far between these days, Kenny."

We were setting the last auto rack in place and I told him what we needed. "Give me about five here, George."

He clicked his radio button. "Pull it five inches, Paddy."

The locomotive engineer delicately pulled back, until George told him, "Good."

That was it, the final rack was properly spaced.

"Thanks, George. Guess I'll see you boys some other..."

A voice on George's radio interrupted me. It was the dispatcher from the tower in the main yard. "Engine 327."

"Come in."

"You fellas are gonna have to sit there for awhile. Two coal trains comin' in are gonna block you."

"10-4."

It really broke my heart that they couldn't leave the ramp. "So, now what do you guys do?"

"Guess I'll sit in the cab with Paddy and stare into space. He ain't much of a talker."

"Ah, hell. Stay here, George. I'll talk to you."

He got on the radio. "I'm stayin' on the ground for awhile, Paddy. It's nice out here."

George's tragic situation had my blood pumping hard. Here was another married fella who seemed a bit neglected at home, an apple ripe for plucking.

I had him softened up mentally, now I had to fix the logistical problem. "Hey, lookee here. Did you see what's in this rack?"

George put his forehead to the side panel and peeked in. "Looks like Caddy's."

"Yep. Brand spankin' new Cadillacs. Wanna check 'em out?"

"Sure."

I got the bolt cutters from my nearby company Jeep and broke the seal on the doors, which was part of my job anyway. Now I'm sure you've seen auto racks in trains when you've been waiting at a crossing. They're completely enclosed by steel plates so tight that sometimes you can't even tell whether there's automobiles inside or not. Once I had the door open, I coaxed George to follow me. "C'mon. Let's inspect the ones on the top level. There's more room up there."

This was true. Head space was limited on the bottom two floors, but on top you could almost stand upright. George followed me up the ladder, mimicking me when I reached the rung even with the third floor and swung my body inside the rack.

"Look at those beauties, George. Fleetwoods."

Even though Cadillac had trimmed the body sizes a bit in response to the onslaught of economical foreign cars, the Fleetwood was still a monster, four door luxury car. I walked down to the middle of the rack and picked out a pretty one. (They were all gorgeous – even in the dim light from the ramp streaking through narrow cracks of the railcar).

Opening the driver's door, I prodded him to partake. "Try this one out. See what it feels like to sit in the driver's seat of a mansion on wheels."

George jumped in with the enthusiasm of a teenager, acting like he was up to some no good prank. As he settled into his seat, I slipped around the front bumper and took my place on the passenger's side.

The smell of brand new leather permeated my nostrils, stirring my blood up even more. "Take a deep breath, George. It's like heaven in here."

He leaned back in the cushy seat and filled his lungs. That bulky chest puffed up so thick, I could see the tips of his nipples pushing out on the shirt fabric. "Man, that is one sweet smell."

"Kinda turns me on, George. Maybe if you bought your wife one of these, she'd be a little nicer to you."

He sarcastically laughed. "Yeah. Maybe I'd just throw her in the back seat and fuck her brains out."

I wasted no time. "Too bad your wife's like that. It ain't right that a fella can't get his dick taken care of when he needs it."

"I just gotta jack it 'til she's ready."

"The smell of this car makes me wanna jack mine right now."

"Well, shit. I got nothing else to do. I'll just join you."

Gee, that was easy. Within seconds, our jeans were unsnapped and unzipped with two puds wild and free. He didn't seem overly curious as to why mine was already hard as could be, but kept his eye on me as he worked on his. He struggled to get started and I kind of felt sorry for him.

"Need some help?" There it was. I said it. He could either thump me on the head with whatever weapons were handy, bolt from the car in disgust, or be sensible and let me take over for him. He chose number three.

"Sure. Have at it." He removed his hand and left its lifeless mass exposed.

I reached over with my right hand and grasped his meat. As I began to pump his cock in my fist, I strategically rubbed underneath the spongy mushroom head with my fingers. Then, I gave him instructions. "This car is all electric. Start up the motor."

He turned the key and that 350 roared to life.

"Now reach down to your left and lift the front button."

He did as told and the seat back moved towards the back, taking his upper torso with it and giving me room to operate. I lowered my head and took him. Burying his fat meat into my warm, stimulating mouth, I worked my tongue onto the entire surface to get him revved up. He swelled, and within seconds that balloon of his was fully inflated. Like his torso, George's cock was thick, bulky and strong. The length wasn't anything to brag about, but the diameter more than made up for it.

His mighty sausage split my jaw open wide, as I made a gallant attempt to keep my teeth off of him. Being born to worship the male penis – any length, width, shape or whatever, I professionally managed to get my mouth positioned properly to lick, squeeze and slavishly praise this man's tool.

George silently told me I was doing my job well, because he reached up to unbutton his shirt – ok, I'll confess that I gave him the idea by unbuttoning the lower ones myself. Once he had all fasteners undone, he peeled both sides back and exposed his glorious chest and belly to me. Then he folded up his arms and placed them between the back of his head and the Fleetwood's headrest.

Covered with medium thick brown fur, his pectoral muscles bulged with masculine strength, and parked in the middle of each, his glorious nipples were perfectly round and dark brown with tips rising majestically into the air. A wide, singular line of hair was the centerpiece of his stomach. This growth lightened as it approached his navel, while below the oval his manly fur spread in all directions, covering his belly and melding into his heavy brown sprouts of pubic hair.

His belly was a little rounded, probably from drinking beer to forget about his unfortunate home life. That's not a put down. I thought it was adorable, so I pretended that I needed him for leverage and placed my left hand directly over his navel. Although it was rounded, the firm muscle underneath was evident against my palm, so I slowly moved my hand back and forth to cop a better feel and massage that beautiful beach-ball belly of his.

While my right hand slowly worked on me, my mouth savagely worked on him. I took his fat helmet to the back of my throat and held it there, ruthlessly crushing out his blood out while using the back of my tongue to scrape his corona.

The poor man moaned with ecstatic pleasure, then broke the silence some more. "Oh, man. That feels great. Yeah, suck on that big cock, faggot. Suck it good."

Oops. That was something I didn't want to hear. Now, I know beggars can't be choosers, but I have never begged. Besides, I have a real problem with guys calling me names when I'm trying to make them feel good. I realize that sometimes it is merely a means for them to motivate themselves and I shouldn't take it personally, but to me, if your cock is in my mouth, I'm the one in control and you should just shut the fuck up and enjoy it. If you wanna talk, then you should be the dominant partner of the action.

So, not wanting to hear this shit in this situation, I schemed for a scenario whereby he could be just that – the dominator. I drew back my lips and licked the head of his unit, then released it. "You aren't close, are you?"

He was a little miffed. "Hell, no. You just started."

"You like to fuck, don't you?"

"Yeah."

"Leave it to me. I'm gonna take good care of you."

All of a sudden, he was like a little kid once more. George enthusiastically followed my lead, as we exited the car and stripped down to our socks. After raising the driver's seat back to an upright position, powering down the four windows and turning off the engine, I soon was sitting slouched down in the middle of the cushy and cavernous back seat, while George stood on the floor in front of me, bent at a 90 degree angle and steadying himself with both hands clamped into the leather seat back by the rear window.

Pointing to my mouth, I leaned forward and turned the festivities over to him. "Here you go, George. Fuck this."

I took his excited penis inside me, moved my lips midway onto his pulsating shaft and waited. George brought his hips forward and rammed that meat into my throat. I opened up wide and let him in, holding my head steady and allowing him to be the aggressor.

Soon, his instincts took over and he fucked my mouth with gusto. Digging his fingers into the curve of the leather seat back, George ruthlessly drove his powerful pecker into the depths of my warm saliva pit, dominating me like the man he was meant to be. Now he could talk all he friggin' wanted to.

"God damn, you're hot. Eat this, cock sucker. Ooh... mmmph. Feels so fuckin' good."

George was a pro, just like I figured he'd be. At first, I let him get his rhythm going, as he ruthlessly poked and swivelled his hips, ramming that thick cock into me from every angle, but once his groove was on, I put my talents to good use. I chomped down on his big strong cock. Bad ass George had the guts to drive his dick to the back of my throat with no problem, so I clamped shut my jaw when he got there, just to see if he had the guts to pull himself out of my trap. He did, but was tortured in doing so. My tongue and roof of mouth locked him in their vise, causing him to shudder, nearly causing him to collapse upon retraction.

That's right, George. No more freebies, George, you half-man half-gorilla. I'm gonna torture you good from now on, because once I clamp onto a man's cock there's no escape until you give me what I want. Doesn't matter if you're coming or going, my mouth's locked onto you for good. If you wanna shoot in my mouth, you're gonna have to suffer for it, you fucking Neanderthal you.

My motivational was with thought, because I had a dick in my mouth. George said his aloud, once he knew what was happening to him. "Aw, Jesus... oh, god damn, that is tight..." as he gallantly drove his plow through my defenses, all the way to the depths of my throat.

That's right, George talked up a storm, but from then on most of his talking was done with animal sounds, grunts, groans, undefinable noises of pain and pleasure. Best of all, our battle made him sweat. Beads surfaced to glimmer in the shards of light poking through our metal-plated auto rack. Beads multiplied to layers of sweat, a slick lathering that matted the hairs of his chest, belly and arms. George worked his ass off, because I made him. I made him be what I wanted him to be, my dominating ape-man, my skull-fucking gorilla man, and once I had him worked up into a sweat-drenched frenzy, I got a feel of what I'd created. I reached up behind me and put my hands to his chest. With George violently thrusting his torso to and fro, his slick-wet chest raced along the palms of my hands, saturating me with manly sweat.

It should have been enough for me. It would have been enough with most men who've fallen into my clutches, but something about George said, "punish me." His powerful fuck, his masculine muscle and fur, his dripping onto me sweat all combined to demand I heighten his pleasurable pain, and so I grabbed each of his tits between fingers and thumbs and held on for the ride. My arms were free to move in unison with his to and fro chest, while I lightly pinched and twisted those gorilla-like nipples, and George grunted like one with short, deep, guttural tones each time he drove his cock towards me. "Uh... ah... mmph... argh."

As his thrusts and grunts increased pace and intensity, I let go his tits and slid off the seat. Kneeling on the floor between his massive thighs, I forced George to poke a hole through the back of my neck. No room for him to retract now, his thrusts were short, deep and quick, and they came from every angle. His sweat-soaked belly slammed against my forehead. His dangling, sperm-filled nuts bounced against my chin, until I grabbed hold of them. That's right. I twisted his monkey nuts while he fired his load directly down my hatch.

George didn't make any more animal sounds. He cried out like a man who'd lost everything dear to him. He drove that fat cock deep into my throat, but this time did not resist my clamping vise. He stayed right there and I held him tight, as his tasty sperm rocketed into me like bullets, and once I knew I had him, I took over.

My lips mercilessly pressed into his wet pubes, and then withdrew. My tongue scraped the shit out of his cock all the way to his pulsating mushroom head. I crushed his contracting peter between my roof of mouth and wet-sandpapered tongue, violently fucking myself with the same dominating power he had used to do it himself. And in my fingers, his tortured nuts were twisted and pinched, as they desperately released their bounty. George twitched. He spasmed. He nearly collapsed atop me, but I gave him no mercy. I sucked on him like I was scraping dry paint. I crushed his fat cock until it was nothing more than a toothpick.

Skull-fuck me, will ya? Fine, mister, but I ain't letting you go until I'm finished. I don't care if you friggin' pass out on me... I'm taking it all. You hear me? Give me everything you got, you fucking super-charged he-man fuck machine.

That's what I told myself. That's what I did. George held on, his grunts downgraded to whimpers, and I do believe that if not for the Fleetwood's seat back holding him up, he may very well have collapsed to crush me beneath his massive, rock solid body. My finishing of him came about with no forethought, just a natural reaction to a natural male animal, my railroadin' man, George.

So, his healthy tool was orally squeezed, licked dry, and mercifully released. In his taxing performance, poor George had created a bit of a problem for both of us. His sweat, streaming from his pores like an untamed river, had and still were dotting the brand new leather of a rather expensive car for which we both were responsible. Funny that this struck fear into me more than if we'd been caught with George's dick fucking my mouth. "C'mon, George. Let's get out of here."

We piled out of the back seat and quickly dressed. "What are we gonna do about that mess?" He wanted to know.

"Don't worry. I got something that'll clean it, but I better hurry before it dries up on me." This was said to alleviate him from guilt. After all, I was the one who'd chosen this wheeled castle for our scene of activity.

With that said, George seemed pretty well satisfied with what had just happened to him. "God damn, that was good stuff."

"Just think, George, now you can say you've fucked someone in the back of a Cadillac."

"Yeah. That was tighter than any pussy I can remember." He looked at the car, still concerned. "You think anyone'll find out?"

I knew what he was getting at. He wanted to know that *if* the damage was unfixable and *if* someone asked the night watchman about it, *how many* out of two men were planning to take the heat.

"Everything will be fine, George. I'll inspect it and fix 'er up. I got nothing else to do all night. And if I can't. I'm the only one who has access to these auto racks. Right?"

"Thanks Kenny." The good-natured fist I'd given to him earlier was now given by him to me. "I better get back to the cab. Paddy's probably jackin' *his* meat by now."

We both headed down the ladder and I bid him farewell, "See ya next time, George."

While engine 327 sat on the ramp at the far end of my auto racks, I spent the next hour or so getting the Fleetwood back to new, using leather treatment I kept in my car, which just happened to be an older Cadillac, a two door coupe with the 425 engine from the late 1970's.

I never did anything overly exciting in the back of my Caddy, but I sure have a nostalgic fondness for big ol' Fleetwoods. That leather treatment worked like a charm. Not a trace of George's manly sweat remained in the Fleetwood, but it permeated my nostrils for many hours to come.

PART TWO – PADDY'S TURN

After getting the Fleetwood cleaned and put back together like new, I climbed down the ladder and headed for the company Jeep, intending to return the cleaning materials to my car outside the fenced in ramp. Getting to the Jeep was no easy task, however.

The racks were brought in and set on two rails – one for railcars filled with new automobiles to be off-loaded; the other for empties, which would be loaded with outbound pickup trucks. All this would happen on the day shift.

These two rails were about 10 feet apart and the line of empties stood between me and the Jeep, staggered with the loaded line behind me where the Fleetwoods were. I needed to go to the nearest space between two empties, climb over the couplers and then I could get back to my Jeep. As I reached an opening and rounded the corner of the rack, a man was leaning on the couplers and facing me with arms folded.

I stopped dead in my tracks, like I'd seen a ghost, because for a second or two, that's what I thought it was. Besides that, there wasn't supposed to be anyone inside that fence besides me and the crew of engine 327.

"Hey, mister. Who are you and what d'ya want?"

"Hi, Kenny. I'm Patrick. They call me Paddy." He held out his hand for a shake.

After breathing a sigh of relief, I clasped his hand. "Jesus Christ, Paddy. You scared the shit out of me. You should have hollered or somethin', so I'd know you were out here."

"Sorry. George said to come on down."

"You run the 327, right?"

"Yep."

"You sure know how to touch and go on your coupling."

"Thanks."

"So, what's up? Still blocked?"

"George said you might want to help me with my problem."

I knew where he was headed with this, but I wanted to hear him ask for it. "Oh, yeah? What problem is that?"

He stood up and placed a hand on his crotch, then gave it a rub. There was no smile, no change in demeanor.

"Gotta rash, huh?"

"Yep."

"What do ya think'll cure it?"

"B.J."

Jeez, George hadn't been kidding when he said Paddy wasn't much of a talker. In fact, he had no personality at all, but I figured that would work just fine. I could fully concentrate on whatever was hiding in those Carhartt jeans of his. "Hell, Paddy. I can do that. Whip it on out."

Not a word or smile came from his mouth. He headed down the 10 foot alley between railcars, until he found a spot where dark shadows and the stagger of the racks made us completely hidden from all eyes, including George, who was back in the cab of the 327.

Still silent, Paddy found his spot. Then, he removed his boots, followed by his shirt, pants and underwear. Right before my eyes and unannounced, this stoic, no-nonsense and horny guy stripped down to his white socks, then just stood there exposed and waited.

As my eyes adjusted to the darkness, I could see this tall, lanky fellow's body. Standing around 6'2" with arms hanging at his sides, Paddy's chest, waist and legs formed a nearly straight line. There were very few curves anywhere and the only body hair I could detect were the pubes. His skin was white as milk and almost glowed in the dark shadows of our canyon.

I bundled up the rag I'd used for cleaning, knelt to the asphalt and placed the rag under my knees for cushion. Using my thumb and forefinger, I grabbed some skin on top of his cock and lifted it to meet my mouth. I sucked on his flaccid meat like it was a baby bottle, using my tongue to stimulate the underside, hoping to give it life. Mission accomplished. Paddy's swelling started with his width. Then, his mushroom head came at me as his cock length increased inside my warm and wet mouth. Further and further, deeper and deeper, this man's cock invaded me and I began to wonder when he would reach full erection. I was forced to draw back in an attempt to keep my stimulation focused on the head of his organ, as more and more shaft separated my lips from his pelvis.

Like a python, the slithering serpent continued to lengthen, forcing me to lean further and further back. Finally, I was left no choice but to adjust the position of my knees in order to accommodate him. My lips no longer could reach his pubes without his cock head piercing my throat, so I sucked on the outer half, knowing that soon his penis would arrive to full erection. Wrong. The damned thing kept coming forward, forcing me to adjust my knees once again.

What the hell had I gotten myself into? My jaw was still a little stiff from taking George's ram roddin' wanger just over an hour earlier, so I thought I better take a look at what this fella was packin'. Releasing the organ from my mouth, I took a deep swallow of spit and scrutinized what I had wrought.

This guy's cock looked like a goddamned javelin. It was no more than one inch in diameter, but had to be at least 11 inches long – and that is a conservative estimate, which I used to convince myself that I could complete the task at hand. Like the rest of his body, Paddy's cock formed a straight line, while the shape of his mushroom was slender, making it nearly impossible to see the rim. And if I couldn't see it, how the hell could I feel it? Stimulate it? And the menacing organ still wasn't hard, or if it was then it was the kind that sagged. It dangled in a downward curve, waiting for me to test its true potential.

I was hoping Paddy liked to be deep throated, because that was about the only way I'd be able to cure his rash. My reputation was at stake and I was not about to let this bizarre looking alien intimidate me.

My lips returned to him, sliding over the hardly-felt rim and working down on the shaft. 'Little bit at a time, Kenny,' I told myself and that is how I attacked. Paddy stood motionless and silent, while I gradually worked my lips towards him. Curving the tongue, I wrapped his cock like a frank in a bun and began to scrape, nearly managing to encircle its skinny diameter. Inch by inch, I stroked him to and fro, taking him deeper into my throat with each forward thrust. My lips finally returned to the midway point of his shaft, which forced the head of his worm to the very back of my throat. Now, I pushed a little further and felt his snake head invade my curve, entering the portal to my esophagus. I clamped on tight in a frantic attempt to avoid triggering my choke mechanism, then pulled back, swallowed and took him down deeper.

For the first time since I had heard him say "B.J.," Paddy's voice box made a sound – an eerie, high-pitched hiss, so I took him even further. My tongue was no longer able to stimulate the head of this never-ending tube, because it was buried deep into my throat, bent and curving downward inside me, as though it was trying to poke my Adam's apple. Hell, I think maybe it was. Surely to god this evil penis was now fully erect, but I was afraid to spit it out for inspection. I didn't want to know.

But I must say that Paddy's dick effected me like they all do, once I got used to its bizarre shape and size. I loved this slender, impaling straw. Never before had I taken such a gagger this far down my throat, so I thought I'd experiment a little, just to see how bad I could torture this guy. Holding him bent into my throat, I clenched the muscles in my neck, crushing that tubular hot dog to the diameter of a harmless licorice stick.

Another whimper was heard and Paddy's slender body become rigid. Every muscle was tensed, and all of a sudden he became beautiful to me. His sinewy chest and belly had at once become a glorious design of wiry lines and curves. The glow of his white skin juxtaposed against the darkness of our alley, making him appear as some sort of masculine, ghostly figure – a kind of mysterious spirit from another world.

Guess you could say I was getting into it. My worship intensified. I withdrew my lips and brought him out of the depths. Then, I savagely attacked his smooth helmet, crushing, licking and sucking with a frantic ferocity what I knew was there but could not feel. Liking this, Paddy reached up with both arms and placed them behind his head. He arched his back and thrust that serpentine cock forward. Paddy literally tried to pierce the back of my neck with his threatening spear, thus throwing down the gauntlet. Now, the shit was on. Try to gag me, will you? Ya friggin' alien... ya freak from another world.

I plowed my head towards him and took his snake head back to the curve of my throat, forcing him past there to once more invade my neck. This time I crushed the hell out of him. I literally tried to hurt him. I did hurt him, but in a pleasurable way. As I continued to swallow his tubular meat, my lips ant-crawled the length of his shaft, forcing his cock head deeper and deeper down my throat. Paddy was conquered, oh, yes he was. My moist, drooling lips made contact with his pubic hair. I crawled a bit more, pressing my lips to his pelvic bone. That serpentine monster of his was completely mine, totally engulfed. Take that, buddy. You lose, I win... we both win.

The muscles in my neck contracted and squeezed him in my vise. Figuring he wasn't going anywhere, I reached up with my right hand and rubbed underneath his balls with my fingertips, causing a shudder throughout his entire body. I thought I might have to prop him up. His knees were weak, but he was ready. Paddy had reached his limit. He let out a shrill, ghostly moan and I withdrew my lips, wrapped my tongue around the head of his snake and scraped like there was no tomorrow.

This man's venom tasted good. That deadly javelin convulsed and contracted time after time to excrete his seed, as I savagely stroked and attacked the sensitive mushroom head to elicit more. He arched his back even further, driving his spear straight forward while the discharge of his come transformed into an even, flowing stream. I swallowed his meat again, taking it down the curve of my throat and allowing his sperm a straight shot to my belly.

Naturally, Paddy never said a damned thing, but he could not stifle his painful, other-worldly howls of release. His body remained tensed and muscles rigid, while his back arched, hands clamped behind his head. With my fingertips delicately rubbing and coaxing what remained inside his nuts, I crunched on the head of his wiener, keeping it firmly clamped with the muscles of my neck. Then, Paddy was beaten, nothing left to give. Paddy joined my list, another victim, another man rendered a useless rag inside my talented mouth.

Sad to say it, but I wasn't finished with him. I was rough on Paddy. I guess that somehow his sinewy body seemed to invite torment, as though it needed to suffer. Can't explain what made me feel this way, but I wasn't getting any protest, so I worked him over good while he twitched and contorted and whimpered.

Paddy loved it, he wasn't fooling me.

My plan was to work him over until he verbally told me to stop. I wasn't afraid of him and, for some strange reason, he brought out an aggression in me that was unfamiliar. I wanted to torture this guy and force him to talk to me. Only with some offer of human communication would I allow him to remove his cock from my death-grip. Unfortunately for me, and fortunately for him, my plans were rudely interrupted by an unexpected sound.

"Engine 327."

Nearby but out of sight, we heard the voice of George. "Come in."

"About 20 minutes and you're out. I'll clear you a path to the hump."

"Roger."

I let go of Paddy's worm and swallowed a big gob of spit, as George stepped out from the corner of the auto rack, where he had been watching our performance.

Paddy, ever the stoic, just stood naked and silent, so I rose to my feet and asked the obvious. "Hey, George. How long've you been there?"

"About five minutes."

"What'd you think? Look ok?"

"Looked good from where I was standing. What'd you think, Paddy?"

"Real good."

For Paddy that was a mouthful. I kind of felt sorry for George in a way. How in the hell could he be around this dullard for an entire shift night after night without blowing a fuse? Maybe his work partner was the cause of his seemingly low spirits, and not his wife.

I guess he'd just grown accustomed to it, but I actually wanted to slap Paddy down – kind of like Edward G. Robinson used to do in those old movies: 'So, tough guy, eh? Maybe this'll make you talk.' WHACK! Out of respect for George, however, I was pleasant, and besides, George seemed much better now for some reason. I kindly acknowledged Paddy's half-assed compliment. "Well gee, Paddy... you're welcome."

Anyway, now both members of engine 327 were fully satisfied. Right?

PART THREE – HE NEVER SWALLOWS

Now that Paddy and George had both been professionally drained, I felt it was necessary that they understand something.

I didn't want every Tom, Dick and Harry coming into my ramp for a blow job. I'd greedily fixed George because I liked him. I had generously done Paddy because George had sent him to me. Now it was time both of them know that they were members of an exclusive club, so I issued my warning.

"That was fun and all fellas, but let's make something clear. This was for you guys only. I don't want every yokel comin' in from the main yard thinkin' they're gonna get the same treatment. If they do, I'll play like I don't know what the fuck they're talkin' about. I figure you guys are smart enough not to screw up a good thing. Am I right?"

For once, Paddy took the lead. "You got nothing to worry about."

I stood in shock and wonder, as still-stripped Paddy strolled over to George and opened George's belt buckle. Within seconds, George's radio laid on the asphalt and his jeans and underwear dropped to his ankles. George stood with hands on hips, grinning at me.

Paddy took that fat sausage into his mouth, while George waved me over.

I was laughing my ass off. "Jesus Christ, George! No wonder he doesn't talk much."

"How's the Fleetwood look?" George asked as though nothing else was happening.

"Clean as a whistle. Not a spot left."

"Good man." He unbuttoned his shirt and peeled it away, dropping it to the asphalt. "Get over here behind me, Kenny." I did as asked. "You work up here and he'll take care of that down there." Standing behind George, I placed my lips to the crook between his neck and shoulder, kissing him, gently tugging on his soft hairs. George whispered. "Paddy does this to me all the time."

"Then why did you let me get you off?"

"He never swallows. Never finishes. Neither does my wife, for that matter. I was hoping you'd do it right... and I was right about that hunch."

Was he ever. Fucking amateurs. Sliding my arms under his, I buried my hands into George's chest hair. I rubbed up and down, side to side, making sure my thumbs clipped his nipple tips. The soft, fine follicles sprouting from George's shoulder tickled my nose, and I smothered his neck and shoulder with kisses, whispering in between. "I had you figured wrong. I thought you hadn't got off for a long time – that load you gave me said I was right, but I guess not." I shifted to his other shoulder for more kisses, extending my hand rubs to include his hard belly. "God damn, George... our little Fleetwood incident was hot. I ain't ever had a man skull fuck me like you did. That was one helluva thing... shootin' a wad like that. Now, here you are back for more."

"Well, a man my age's gotta take advantage of every opportunity."

George had me hypnotized again. I forgot all about Paddy down there sucking George's dick, but it was convenient to have him there so I could concentrate on my gorilla's chest and belly. As my hands rubbed the tips of his erect nipples, George let out a slight groan. I already knew this was one of his flash points so I lingered there, gently pinching them between finger and thumb.

"God, Kenny. You sure know how to get my motor runnin'," he whispered. "I want you to finish me, ok?"

"Fuck yeah. Just tell me when."

My lips moved to the back of his neck, where no barber had been for far too long. I relished it. The hair here was thick and soft. I clinched tufts of it into my lips, gently tugging and licking. Meanwhile, my hands raced down to his belly, then back up to the chest, where I'd grab those manly nipples, squeeze and return to massage every inch of his furry torso.

George reached up with both arms and placed his hands behind my head, dear soul that he was. Strong-ass son of a bitch stretched himself out for me, inviting more of my neck painting, more of my chest and belly rubbing. He spread his legs a little further apart, then thrust his chest, belly and pelvis forward, offering his torso to me and cock to Paddy, begging us to worship him.

This time, George remained mostly silent. Other than occasional groans of pleasure, his reaction to our assault was a stark contrast to when he had fucked my mouth. No longer an animalistic Neanderthal, he had become a surrendering slab of prime beef, accepting our two-pronged assault with a trance-like ecstasy.

Our combined effort was taking George to a fantasy world – a place only he could know or enjoy.

As my hands reached the lowest part of his firm belly, I squeezed and pressed inward, hugging him there before moving onto his chest to hug him there. After another nipple pinch, my palms did a gradual but hard pressing down the length of his torso, stopping near his bushy pubes where Paddy's forehead made contact with the backs of my hands. His tempo of oral strokes quickened, as he took his lips to pubic hair before withdrawing, his head twisting side to side.

Hot friction is what George needed. He never asked, but my idea was accepted, as I frantically worked my hands in small circles. Pressing hard, I warmed both pectorals, both nipples and the entire surface of his belly. His chest and belly hairs made brushing sounds beneath my palms, as though conductors of electricity. There were sparks, but they were inside George's manly body. Inside, George was feeling very manly. He sucked his abdominal cavity in and further thrust out his chest, arching his back into a dramatic curve. His fingers were tightly locked behind my head and he pulled me closer, forcing me to bury my face deep into the nape of his thick and furry neck.

With his chest and belly afire, I clamped onto his tits. George grunted with unbridled pleasure. His knees weakened and muscles tensed, as he confirmed what I knew was coming with a shout to the man below. "I'm nuttin', Paddy. Look out!"

I prepared to release my nipple pinch and take Paddy's place on George's pulsating cock, but Paddy never moved. He continued to frantically stroke the mighty meat, rapidly sliding his lips forward and back, while turning his head side to side.

George's rockets fired at will. His entire body convulsed and all breathing stopped, as his juicy organ contracted again and again. Paddy never flinched, never broke off his rhythmic pattern of oral strokes, which caused George to twitch and contort. His back arched even more. Impossible, I thought, but my nipple-pinching fingers drew away from me to confirm it. With a mighty groan, George finally exhaled and sent a second wave of orgasmic fluid streaming down Paddy's throat. My hero clamped onto my neck, forcing my face to press so deeply into his neck that I could hardly breathe. But I did breathe in deep and hard, sucking in the manly aroma of dried sweat while continuing to tweak those now-tiny nipples.

George nearly collapsed in my arms, so I removed my nipple pincers and raced the palms of my hands up and down his chest and belly, pressing hard to keep him aloft. With one final jolt, one final burst, George let go my neck, straightened his spine and dropped his head in satisfied exhaustion. His muscular arms hung limp at his sides, while my arms were clamped by his sweaty arm pits, my hands stationary on his chest to keep him aloft. As for Paddy, he finished his job, sucking and licking this man's wonderfully fat peter until it was bone dry.

We drained poor George of everything he had – strength, come and sweat, all were taken from him by our tag team attack. Paddy released George's dick and pecked it with a kiss, while I kept his partner from collapsing to the ground.

George stood there teetering for awhile, then gradually regained his senses, while Paddy rose to his feet and dressed himself.

"You ok, George?" I moved in front to admire his hair-covered, burly physique one final time, as beads of sweat again dotted his masculine fur.

"Yeah, man oh man." George was grinning but still weak, his chest heaving and arms hanging limp. "Thought I's gonna pass out there for a second." He reached down to his ankles, pulled up his underwear and jeans at the same time.

While he put those together, I handed him his shirt. "Hey, George. You've had quite a shift so far tonight."

"You ain't kiddin'. You guys almost killed me that time. Hope we get blocked in here every night."

"Won't bother me none."

"Me neither."

Staying true to form, Paddy had already headed back to the cab, not saying a word to either me or George. Funny thing is, Paddy never did come back to see me on those rare occasions when engine 327 came into my ramp. Never could figure out why. Never did ask George about it. He certainly never missed an opportunity, and we smartly covered with bath towels the back seat of whatever brand new car we used so that George and I could do battle with no worries. I supplied the towels. I supplied the tight mouth for George to fuck. George supplied me with healthy doses of man seed jettisoned from a man who was my ideal. Lots of meat, lots of muscle, lots of fur, George was more animal than man, and when it came time for me to be skull-fucked nobody could do it better.

Sadly, engine 327 and its crew stopped coming into my ramp. Once the new guys from the defunct railroad came in, George and Paddy got reassigned to a small yard on the other side of town and I never saw them again.

I felt ok with it, though. I figured I'd gotten what I wanted out of George and with my help Paddy had lost all fear of George's sperm. I'm sure my pal was properly serviced any time he needed it from that day on.

Don't you believe it. Do you think I didn't exchange phone numbers with that manimal? It is true that I never again saw them at my workplace, but as far as the crew chief of engine 327 is concerned, he found that a bed gives him much more freedom to dominate me like he's supposed to do. And as for me, I discovered that George lit by a bedside table lamp is far preferable to George in near darkness. No towels are needed. Go ahead and sweat all over me, you bad-ass beast.

A MONDAY MILKING FANTASY

PART ONE – DAMNED NAZIS

My pal Curt and I had awakened from our overnighter to a good morning wrestling match in our underwear – nothing serious, just fun and games as usual. He eventually found himself laying on top of me with his back against my chest, at which time he threw back his arms in a show of surrender.

Using my best Nazi accent, I threatened him, "Now, Mr. Nolan, we have given you every opportunity to speak. This is your last chance. Do not force us to torture you."

He immediately recognized the play. Quoting a line directly from the movie we had watched the night before, he growled in a masculine voice. "Get on with it."

Returning to my normal English, I told him what to do. "Curt, let me out from under you. I've got an idea."

I let go his arms and he rolled off me to stand at bedside. We both immediately looked at each others' raging hard-ons, then laughed.

"You want me to strip, Greg?"

"No," I told him. "I'll take care of that soon enough."

I took the two pillows and stacked them in the upper center of the mattress about where my chest had been, then pointed. "Stretch out over those."

Curt draped himself over the pillows chest up and spread his arms and legs into an X, while I stalked around the bed for inspection, which also gave me some time for plotting. The view from above was much better for me. Curt's chiseled chest rose majestically into the air, while his stomach and belly sloped dramatically downward from the end of his rib cage. A well-defined ridge of muscle began in the middle of his stomach and led to his stretched navel, where a fine trail of dark fur began its journey to the pubic hairs. Those I could not see, not yet. "I'm gonna play Nazi again. If you want me to stop, just say 'hornet's nest' and I'll be me again."

"Ok."

Hornet's nest referred to our gymnasium, one of those traditional monikers handed down from one class to the next since its opening.

Reaching the foot of the bed, I grabbed both ankles and stretched his legs taut, pausing to lightly caress the soles of his feet. They were perfectly masculine with high, strong arches and thick, meaty toes. Here, dark brown hairs sprouted on most of them, while a healthy growth had also begun on each instep.

"Say it, so I know you got it, Curt."

"Ok, damn it, hornet's nest."

From this angle, I knew where I had to begin – that gloriously stretched belly just had to be punished, because long ago I'd figured out this was a triggering point for him. Ever since I'd known him, he was always rubbing on it with his hand during casual conversations. In the summertime, if he wasn't shirtless, which was rarely, he wore shortened t-shirts that exposed some or all of his middle section. Besides that, any time I had tried to give him a claw during one of our many fake wrestling matches or simply give him a pink belly for no reason, he would always protest about how he hated when someone touched his belly. This to me meant he secretly wanted to be touched there one way or another.

I went to the closet and retrieved my Louisville Slugger, laid the head of it onto the pit of his stomach and addressed him, once again as a Nazi.

"Now, Mr. Nolan, why were you sent here? What is your mission?"

He looked up over his chest, his eyes following the line of bat from my hand to his stomach, and then lowered his head with a mighty groan. "I'll never tell you."

With a controlled and harmless uplift, I let the head of the wooden bat drop to tap the muscle just below his navel. An explosion of rippling muscle rose to the surface, as he flexed his abdominals in a defensive posture. Another raising with a bit more height produced a little more force, this time landing into the pit of his stomach and causing Curt to strain his arms against imaginary chains. He expanded his chest and emitted a manly grunt as though he'd taken full-blown contact of bat to muscle.

Repeatedly bringing the bat down onto his middle section, I carefully regulated the power of my strokes to make minimal impact. The wood targeted every part of that gloriously stretched and flexed middle from just under his rib cage to just above his pelvic bone. Each time contact was made my victim would grunt or let out masculine "uhhhs" to receive his punishment, while I kept a close eye on his briefs. His rock solid pecker pointed straight down in its cotton prison, which pulled his waistband lower and lower to expose even more of his fur trail. The outlined crown of his unit was clearly visible, as a pre-orgasmic ooze saturated the cloth pocket. Naturally, mine was doing the same thing, also unattended.

He obviously was ready, but I figured we had all day and the longer I pretended to torment him the better would be the end result for both of us. Climbing up on the mattress to kneel beside his chest, I Nazi'd him some more. "Why don't you talk, Mr. Nolan? How much more of this do you think you can take?"

He raised his head to glare at me. "You'll never break me."

"We shall see."

I moved to kneel next to his middle section, then took the handle end of the bat and placed it just below his navel. Slowly, I began to push down and grind it into his belly, all the while continuing the interrogation. "Talk, Nolan. What is your mission?"

Manly groans and grunts spewed from his mouth, while he flexed his chest and further tightened his abdominals. Meanwhile, I increased the pressure, grinding and twisting the blunted end of the bat deeper and deeper into his muscle. His poor cock was doing everything it could to escape those briefs and had grown to the point where his waistband now was pulled past the beginnings of his pubic hair.

"Why were you sent here? Tell us now, damn you."

"Never... I'll... never talk."

With one final thrust, I ground the ball bat into him with some serious effort and I know it had to hurt, but Curt stayed with the game, groaning and grunting with each exhale of breath. Then, I removed the bat from him. He relaxed, breathing heavily with exaggerated raising of his chest on the ins and flattening of his belly on the outs.

"Mr. Nolan, we have tortured you for nearly two hours. Why don't you talk?"

"Torture me all you want. You'll never break me."

I placed one hand on his middle section and began to gently rub. "You are a strong adversary, Mr. Nolan. We have beaten your belly to a pulp, yet you refuse to talk. I hate to tell you this, but there are other ways to break a strong man like you."

My hand drifted a little lower, then nudged his undershorts a bit further down to expose a full compliment of curly brown pubes and the base of his thick cock. He looked up over his chest, then collapsed with a heaving groan. "Oh, god... not that."

I clutched the throbbing penis still trapped in its fabric prison. "Oh, god... YES that."

Squeezing hard on his helpless unit, I shouted the order, "Strip him."

Off the bed I sprang to retrieve a pair of scissors from the desk, then carefully slipped one blade between his inner thigh and stretched undershorts. Curt flinched a bit from the touch of cold metal, but never looked up or protested, other than to remain in character with a pitiful pleading.

"What are you doing to me, you sick bastard?"

I cut the fabric and released his imprisoned penis. It sprang upwards and cast the ruined underwear aside, flipping onto his belly with a dramatic smack. The sight of this organ was a stunning surprise, because it was almost as though I was looking into a mirror. Curt's peter was nearly like my own – same thickness and length, same cut, same size and color of crowned head. Having wished many times that I could suck my own cock, my mouth watered when I saw his.

I yanked what was left of his shorts from underneath him and threw them to the floor, then slowly paraded around the bed to further ready him.

"Look at yourself, Mr. Nolan. Stripped of everything, chained and helpless, your entire body is at our mercy."

I took in the view from the side. His mighty chest rose high into the air, while his middle section dropped like a cliff. To further dramatize the scene, my prisoner pretended to struggle against his chains by arching his back, breathing rapidly and deeply to further display his feigned dread of what was to come. His impressive penis lay throbbing with its slit resting on the lower ridge of his belly button, where pre-cum dribbled into the depths of the navel itself.

I moved to the end of the bed. "Think you are quite the man, don't you Mr. Nolan?" I climbed up to kneel between his spread open thighs. "We will see how much man you are. We will drain you again and again, until you beg us to stop."

Hearing these words caused his scrotum to clinch, which forced his penis to raise an inch into the air and stand at attention for a few seconds before slamming back down. As I grabbed the base of his cock and encircled it with two fingers and thumb, he raised his head with eyes glazed, halfway smiled and tempted me to begin. "Do your worst, you Nazi swine."

I brought his pulsating pole to a vertical stance and wrapped my lips around the mushroom head. Inch by inch, I took his manly meat deeper into my mouth, making sure to keep my tongue scraping the underside of the crown. His writhing and groaning intensified, as I slowly worked my lips towards the manually-formed ring. Once the goal was reached, I removed my fingers and thumb. From here, I would subdue this mighty tool strictly with lips and tongue.

This left both my hands free to fulfill my longtime ambition – to do to him what he professed to hate. Using my palms, I planted them onto his middle section rubbed while reversing direction with lips and tongue to glide up his long pole.

Instantly, Curt reacted. He flexed his chest and further flattened his middle, then raised his head to watch me work him over. "Uhhh... not my belly."

He collapsed his head and continued to writhe and flex. In my peripheral vision was movement, and the scraping of skin against skin confirmed that he was bending back his toes and arching his manly feet. My belly rub pressed down harder and harder. As for the throbbing tool in my mouth, I nearly swallowed the bulging head, stopped to lick and scrape, then began a rhythmic stroking from the base to the top.

Quickly and without warning, I removed my hands from his stomach and reached back to attack his feet. My nails ruthlessly scraped his soles, causing his entire body to shudder. He curled his toes forward to defend himself, thickening their leathery toughness. Now focused on his feet, he was totally unprepared when I brought both hands down full bore onto his belly and dug my fingertips in deep. His muscles were not tightened until it was too late, and my belly impalement sent a mighty surge rippling through the entire length of his cock, a vibration powerful enough to press my tongue and roof of mouth.

This combination was driving the boy mad, so I increased the pressure on his middle section and intensified my oral strokes.

His eyes were closed and head turning side to side, as deep, breathy groans drifted upwards from the bed. Then, the writhing stopped and his entire body tensed. Every muscle flexed to capacity and with a tortured "Oh, my god," he gave his semen to me – not in an explosive way, but more like the foam that spews from a shaken bottle of beer.

Creamy streams gently flowed into my mouth and down the hatch, as I relentlessly continued with my oral strokes and devastating double belly claw.

Curt violently exhaled and arched his back, lifting himself well above the double-stacked pillows. His head was turning side to side and toes curling forward and back. Every muscle was flexed to capacity, while those amazing testicles gave healthy doses of their seed to me. Then, he brought his hands to his chest and rubbed his palms over the tips of his erect nipples, all the while continuing to moan about "my poor belly... oh, my god... oh, my god."

I kept stroking and clutching, until finally he collapsed back to the pillows and resumed his stretched X position. Unfazed, I continued to knead his abdominals, while slurping and scraping his spent penis. He was mercilessly drained of his fluids and soon was flinching from the sensation of post orgasmic pain and pleasure.

I kept waiting for him to say those end the fantasy words of hornet's nest, but he continued saying those please continue words in reference to his tortured belly. A small victory for him, because even though he wanted me to continue, I didn't want to. Curt had fired his first salvo, yet he stayed in the torture rack position as though the game had left him wanting more. Since I was still hornier than I'd ever been before, I was more than happy to remain a Nazi. I licked his peter clean, released my double claw and returned his fading unit to my hand before laying it gently to rest on his fur trail. We'd just see how much he truly wanted to take.

PART TWO – SILLY VOICES

This big event was the culmination of several weeks' worth of buildup. Curt and I had been introduced by a mutual friend, who just happened to have one of the finest in town, half-court set ups for basketball a fella could ever need. The concrete slab was near the garage at his house. One day I dropped by unannounced to see my friend playing a game of "h-o-r-s-e-o-u-t" with this stranger and I liked what I saw, so I introduced myself.

"Hey, Johnnie. What's goin' on?"

"Hi. Just playin' a little b-ball with Curt here."

"Hi Curt, I'm Greg. Who's winning?"

"It ain't even close. One more letter and he's history. "

He dribbled the ball a couple of times, turned to shoot and banked it in off the backboard. Curt had on blue cotton gym shorts, white socks and black Nike high tops. The shirt he had worn was laying in the nearby grass. His shorts were worn low on the waist, which fully displayed that area of interest to me.

"Well, Curt, when you finish him off we'll have a three-way."

Johnnie tried to duplicate the shot, but missed. "Lost again. You two go ahead. I need a break."

He promptly went into the house – jealous maybe. Actually, Johnnie wasn't much of an athlete, even though his dad wanted him to be. He just never took any interest and always welcomed an excuse to do something else. Besides, I liked him for other reasons, one of which was being perceptive enough to suspect what I was up to.

"Wanna horse or one on one, Greg?"

"You call it. It's your court now."

"How 'bout a one-pointer to 10?"

"No. I prefer a two-pointer to 20."

"It's the same damn thing."

I was already laughing, so he knew I was full of crap.

"You asshole," he laughed with me.

"Ok, Curt, one-pointer, take it in."

It was mostly casual at first. I had a respectable game and answered every shot he made, but my main focus was to have my hand on him when he went up for a jump shot. Slick with sweat, Curt's chest and hard stomach felt good under my fingertips as he raised up to fire. It soon became apparent that I was better than he, so I kinda let him win the first game. As my reward, he began to belittle and razz me about his superiority, so I upped the intensity to easily win the second and third games, which seemed to piss him off a little.

"You lucky piece of shit. God, I can't shoot today for nothing."

"So, you're saying I ain't any good. It's all about you."

He cracked a smile. "Nah, you're pretty good. I just usually do better."

That's when I first noticed that he kept rubbing his belly as we talked. I figured I'd like to have a go at it too, so I set us up for some intimate contact.

"Maybe you'd do better at wrestling. How 'bout that?"

"You're on."

We headed over for the grass and got into a clinch, then I let him put me into a headlock. As a counter-measure, I formed a claw with my hand and ground it into the perimeter of muscle around his navel.

"God damn, I hate that. Let go."

"Let me outta the headlock."

"No way."

"Then suffer."

So, the shit was on. We both kept our holds clamped firm and I enjoyed having my face buried into his sweaty chest, although my head was throbbing a bit. With one hand on the small of his back and the other digging into his belly, the pressure on him was rather intense. This is when I noticed the boner he had in his shorts. I knew right then and there we would be great friends.

Over the next couple of weeks there were several get-togethers either at his house or mine. We got to know each other pretty good and found some mutual interests, but every hook up would culminate into a wrestling match with the same result – two hard-ons.

Funny thing is he asked me to sleep over with him before I asked him to sleep over with me. He picked a Friday night, which was not good, because his whole family would be home the next day, but a few interesting things did happen when it was time for lights out.

We were in his bed, laying on our backs and quietly talking the usual nonsense in the darkness, when he asked me if I liked to have my back scratched. I said, "Sure," and immediately rolled onto my stomach. He peeled back the covers and went to work with his nails lightly caressing me. Then, he began to use his fingers and turned it into a full-blown body massage. Again we were in our briefs, but I could feel his hard dick under the fabric each time it accidently touched me somewhere. Mine was rock solid, too, crushed under my belly.

It was during this massage that he first used a silly, high-pitched and effeminate voice... "G r e g o r y, you are so handsome. I just love to touch you all over."

After a moment of contemplation, I replied in the same style.

"C u r t i s, I just love when you put your big strong hands all over me."

This was a good scenario. Using these voices made it ok for us to pretend to be queer, which meant we could touch without offending. It put us both at ease with what we were feeling and doing for one another.

That night ended with me returning the massage favor to him, then we pulled up the covers, pulled down our briefs and simultaneously jacked ourselves off. I thought about asking if he wanted me to assist him with the beating of his meat, but decided he would have to ask me first, which is exactly what he did.

"G r e g o r y, if you help me down there, I'll help you."

"Oh, C u r t i s, let's help each other at the same time, ok?"

I buried my head under the covers and worked my way around so my head was at his feet, then I put my right hand on his dick and he put his on mine. With us both laying on our backs, he managed to shoot his load first, which allowed me to get my right hand massaging one of his feet. Soon afterwards, I expelled my load.

After the Kleenex cleanup, we put our shorts back on and fell asleep, never touching each other again until morning, when I was awakened by him putting me in his famous headlock.

The wrestling match was on and we both had erections. He saw mine stretching my briefs and I saw his. We both stopped, looked at each other, smiled and continued the match. His bedroom was in the basement and beyond the door we heard his little brother turn on the TV for Saturday morning cartoons, so we couldn't take our game much further.

On the other hand, I had planned the sleep over at my place far better – a Sunday night. Next morning the house was ours, with both my mom and dad at work and sister having spent the night with one of her friends.

We had repeated the same routine in my bed the night before and again woke up to a wrestling match. Our grappling had taken us from my bed to the floor and back to the bed, when somehow Curt ended up on top of me with his back pressed against my chest. All of a sudden, he threw his arms past the head and relaxed his body, while lovingly calling my name. The silly voice told me we were ready to take another step forward.

Here I had to make a very important decision: I could attack his vulnerable body violently, which would trigger resumption of the increasingly erotic wrestling match; or I could attack him with a soft caress, which would trigger something more exciting. I chose number two.

"Oh, C u r t i s, you are so big and strong." Both my palms made circles on his expanded chest and I made sure to create a little friction across the tops of his stretched nipples.

"Oh, G r e g o r y, you make me feel so manly."

I gently slid my hands down onto his flattened stomach, then belly. He flinched a little, but soon his body again relaxed and he allowed me to put my hands all over him from chest to pelvic bone. I could sense him becoming more aroused, as he began to thrust his chest upwards and further stretch himself. He seemed to be surrendering himself, practically begging for me to do something dramatic.

The problem is that I couldn't see what I was touching. I was smothered underneath with the back of his head near my chin, causing me to turn my head to one side. This of course limited what I could do to please him.

Now, when one fella is testing the waters with another fella, sometimes there's no way to plan or think out what's going to happen. All I knew is that I had to keep him in this position, but figure out a way for me to gain full access to him in this position. A movie we had watched the night before flashed through my brain and that's how I solved it.

Those damned Nazis had tortured this poor British guy and I'd noticed a bit of a bulge in my pal's jean shorts, so I brought my legs up over his to pin his feet, then grabbed his biceps and pulled them down to further stretch him. This is when I became a Nazi for the first time, which culminated into orgasm number one.

Despite the fact that I had just drained his nuts. Curt remained stretched out over the two pillows, ready for more. Things were just starting to heat up.

"Did you think we were finished with you, Mr. Nolan? No, my friend, we have only begun. Let us see how well you perform for us. You will answer our questions soon... or suffer for hour after hour."

I knelt beside his chest, then reached down with both hands and rubbed my palms across his nipples.

"What are these for? So exposed and defenseless, I think we will play with them for awhile to see what happens."

Curtis had the type of tits that were barely visible when he stood upright because they were parked under well-developed pectoral muscles, but with him draped over the pillows and arms laying beyond his head, Curt's tits were magnificently stretched, round and available. As I stimulated them, the tips began to rise high into the air. To my amazement, it seemed that the entire surface of each was becoming a tip until they extended nearly one half of an inch above his chest. Meanwhile, his slumbering penis instantly reacted to my touch, soon again ballooning to reach for his belly button.

With the thumb and forefinger of my right hand, I lightly pinched and twisted his left tip. Then, I put my lips onto his right nipple and began sucking on it like a straw. In between, I'd remove my lips long enough to taunt him.

"What is this? One should not touch a man here. It is only for women. It is humiliating for a man to have his tits abused this way."

He raised his head to curse me. "You sick, sadistic fuck."

I continued pinching and sucking. "Look at these poor, defenseless tits. Am I making them sore? Only you can stop your torment. You must talk."

"Never... no, never... nothing will break me."

"Don't you feel shame? So helpless? So alone... all these eyes ogling over your masculine physique? How does it feel to have your entire body stripped naked before us? Every inch of your powerful body at our mercy? Answer the questions. Why were you sent here?"

"You sadistic bastard." He arched his back to thrust his nipples higher into the air, inviting me to further torment them. "Do what you will. I'll never talk."

His cock was bouncing up and down on his belly in a frenetic dance, as my nipple stimulation sent testosterone levels inside him sky high. My prisoner was feeling as though he were the manliest man in the world, and in our fantasy world of Nazi torture he was exactly that. Raising the intensity, I released both nipples and positioned myself with both knees on top of his abdomen, then I resumed my attack on the erect tips, reversing to suck on the left and pinch the right.

He was taken to dizzying heights, now with my weight crushing his belly and the tantalizing nipple torture combining to drive him to ecstatic madness. Deep, husky groans and breathy uhhh's rumbled from the depths of his chest, while he kept his eyelids shut, locked deep into our fantasy.

"You are very strong, Mr. Nolan. But your powerful muscles cannot help you now."

I ruthlessly sucked on his left tip as though it were a baby bottle, while twisting and turning the right like a radio knob.

Between the calves of my legs, I could feel his helpless peter dancing out of control, smearing pre-come syrup onto any surface it touched.

"We have taken from you everything that makes you a man. It belongs to us. You belong to us. Will you talk?"

"Never."

"Very well... torture his penis!"

Suddenly, I leapt off him and knelt between his thighs. Within seconds, I had thrust his cock into my mouth and assigned each hand to work on his nipples, twisting and turning their elongated tips. Keeping his organ in my mouth and taking it with me, I lowered my forehead onto his stretched belly and pressed down hard, forehead into muscle, then performed my baby bottle suck on his pulsating cock.

My lips were midway on the shaft of this impressive tool, while my tongue ruthlessly licked and scraped the underside of his glorious mushroom head. More and more pressure was put into his belly and onto his tits, as I intensified my three-pronged attack.

Again I saw him draw up his arms and thrust his chest high into the air. I felt the belly being sucked in, as he invited – no, begged me to punish him. I had elevated him to the status of super-hero – stripped naked, chained and ruthlessly assaulted. His masculinity was under attack and he gloriously displayed this manly physique to defy his tormentors. He further stretched his body and raised his chest to intensify his belly and nipple torture, while the pinnacle of his manhood – his increasingly powerful cock – was relentlessly brutalized by lips and tongue.

Strangely, he remained mostly silent during this ordeal. An occasional deep, breathy groan was all that I heard, as my victim drifted deep into his fantasy of being a chained superman, defiantly standing up to the sadistic humiliation and cruelty of his tormentors.

Again, his breathing stopped and muscles tensed to capacity, as another salvo of rich semen foamed into my mouth. His cock was a giant straw from which I sucked out the thick come like it was malted milk – hot, manly, sweet-tasting milk.

Curtis writhed and flexed in orgasmic heaven, while his thick fluid flowed gently from that throbbing tube. It was almost as though the first event had never taken place, but at that age testicles can make plenty of seed whenever their master calls on them to do so.

As before, I continued extracting and stimulating as though nothing new had happened, fully satisfied to work him over until he stopped me. Eventually his body collapsed and his chest heaved, but he remained positioned in his torture rack and allowed me to finish my job.

Occasionally, his body would convulse from the painful, yet pleasurable torment I put on the head of his penis, but not a word was said or defensive motion made – until all of a sudden, he brought his hands to mine and coaxed me to release his tits. He sprang to a seated position and took our game in a new direction.

"Look here, Nazi. I have broken my chains. Now it is your turn to suffer."

As I released his cock from my mouth, he wrapped his legs around my waist and locked me into a crushing body scissors. Then, he rolled to his left and took us both to the floor, where he proceeded to yank my underpants down to my knees.

"Get on your back, you Nazi bastard."

I laid out spread eagle for him and he finished removing my shorts. Immediately, he took my hardened cock into his mouth and started giving me the baby bottle suck. I was instantly mesmerized. This unexpected pleasure had come about so quickly that I had no time to analyze, protest, or do anything other than enjoy it. With burning visions of my tortured hero on the rack still fresh in my memory, I began shooting wads of come into his mouth in less than a minute. He was given fair warning by my forceful exhale of air and tensing from head to toe. If that didn't tell him, my words did. "Oh, man, here I come." Curt didn't care. He never flinched or choked. Rather, he drained me with the expertise of a seasoned pro. Of course, I didn't know what a seasoned pro felt like at the time, but it was the event – the new discovery that ranks this as one of my all time favorite orgasms.

After thoroughly satisfying me and licking my penis dry, he finally ended our game.

"Hornet's nest."

PART THREE – THE 180 DEGREE TURN

We laughed and relived all that had just happened, then realized we both needed to piss. Simultaneous streams splattered into the toilet water as we each admired one another's handsome peters.

"Damn, Curtis, I can't believe our cocks look like twins."

"Yeah, who woulda guessed it?"

He finished first and grabbed some tissue to wipe off the droplets. I did the same and moved close to him as we faced one another. Cupping my dick in hand, I held it out horizontal and grabbed his. We maneuvered closer together and compared ourselves side by side, my cock head buried into his pubes and his buried into mine.

"Hah! Mine's longer," he boasted.

"No it ain't, Curtis. My slit's touching your pubes like yours is mine. They're exactly the same... same width, too, looks to me."

"Yeah, you're right. Wonder whose is bigger when we've got hard-ons."

"We'll have to check it later. I need a break. Guess I owe you a pair of underwear, huh?"

"Damn right, Gregory, you sure do. Just give me an old crummy pair. It doesn't matter. What time is it, anyway?"

"Dunno. You hungry?"

"Big time."

I got him a pair of shorts and checked the time to see it was 11:30. After

I put on my underpants, we went to the kitchen and cooked us some bacon and eggs, while we talked about mundane subjects unrelated to recent events, but very much related to future possibilities.

"When do your parents get home, Greg?"

"One at four thirty and one at five. My sister could come home sooner, but I doubt it. Her friend's mom usually takes them swimming all day when she stays over there."

"I want your dick inside me."

After I somehow avoided choking on a mouthful of eggs, I sat back and looked at him with amazement.

"What?"

"You know, in my crack."

This was a bit of a bombshell and it took me awhile to recover. "Wow, Curt, I don't know. Have you ever done it?"

"No, but there's only one way to find out what it's like. I figure your dick oughtta fit the bill."

"I've never done it either. You sure I ain't too big? What if it hurts you?"

"Hell, if I don't like it I'll take it out. I kinda got it planned to where I can control it I think. I saw in Hustler where this chick was sitting on top of the guy. I think that might work."

"Ok, I'll just lay there and let you do your thing."

I never dreamed he'd want to go there. Frankly, at that time in my life I found the thought of it a bit disgusting, because I always imagined my dick coming out of someone's hole with shit all over it. Like Curtis, however, I figured there was only one way to find out.

We finished eating and cleaned up the mess, then headed to the bathroom for supplies. Having discovered my favorite masturbation lubricant to be baby oil, I kept a bottle of it in my bedroom. Other than that, I suspected we might need a towel or two, so I got some older hand sized ones and asked Curtis if he thought he'd need anything else. He couldn't think of anything, so we returned to my bed and stripped.

It didn't take us long to get fired up again, just a little kissing and hand rubbing on his chest and belly did it for me. My touch revved him up and we were all set.

After returning the pillows to their rightful spot at the head of the mattress, Curtis guided me to lie on my back. He opened the baby oil and lubricated my cock with his hand, then transferred what was left to his asshole. I laid there quietly with hands tucked behind my head, waiting. He straddled me with knees on either side of my hips, grabbed my penis and held it vertical.

My cock head made contact with his ass, and then there was some intense pressure as he forced me past the entry to his rectum. His eyes clenched. His mouth contorted, initial reactions to this first-time invasion, but soon a mischievous smile consumed Curt's face as he slowly accepted me and lowered himself onto my hardened cock. Once he'd slid himself halfway down, he let go with his hand and took me inside as deep as I could go. His buttocks rested on my pelvis and his rectal muscles gradually relaxed.

"What's it like having me in there, Curt?"

"Feels like I gotta shit."

"Does it hurt?"

"Not really. Just feels like I'm gonna explode a big turd."

I cracked up, but tried not to jiggle to much. "That's my turd in there. Looks like your dick's still hard, too."

"Yeah. Wonder what that means?"

"Must mean you like it. You're in charge. I'm just here to be your tool."

He raised his buttocks a few inches, then slid back down. "Hmm, that's kinda nice."

"I agree."

Feeling more relaxed and confident, he gradually began to ride up and down on my thick pole. Using his legs to lift, Curt brought his ass a little higher each time until the upward strokes put the rim of his anus in contact with the rim of my cock head.

This caused a contortion on both our faces – not from pain, but from the newly found pleasures of intercourse. Just when we had a good rhythm going, he slammed his butt cheeks onto me and sat there, squeezing the muscled innards of his rectum.

I groaned with sheer delight, as my throbbing pecker got the life crushed out of it. Then, he wiped the oil off his hand and lifted from me just a bit.

Without a word, Curt made an incrementally slow, 180 degree spin on my cock, carefully keeping me inside while lifting one of his legs to join the other, sitting on me sideways. He turned again, lifting his leg until sitting with his back towards me. Reaching down between his legs with one hand, he forked two fingers to keep my dick inside him while leaning back to lay with his back on my chest.

"You still in there, Greg?"

"Can't you tell? Of course I am."

"Thought so. This is wild. I can't even describe how good this feels."

He brought his arms back and put his ankles together, legs inside of mine. Curt had arrived at his desired position, the same position from where we had begun our sexual escapades, his body stretched atop mine, his chest high, belly low, only this time my pulsating cock was buried deep inside his ass.

"Oh, man, this is too fucking hot," Curt moaned with sheer pleasure. "Your dick feels so damn good in there."

He was squeezing the life out of my pecker and I relished every second of it. With my hands free, I figured it was time for me to become a bit more involved.

"Can you reach the oil, Curt?"

"Yeah, I think so."

"Grease up your pecker."

He grabbed the bottle with his right hand. After squirting some oil onto his cock, he closed and cast the bottle aside, then manually stroked himself. Again the muscles inside him went bonkers, which further crushed my swollen tool.

"Don't jack it off yet. Dry your hand and put both of 'em under my head, if you can."

He could. His youthful body did whatever he asked it to do, as he stretched his arms beyond his head, bending his elbows to tuck both hands beneath my raised head. I lowered to pin him between the pillows and the back of my head. Curt again was my prisoner, gloriously stretched chest-up across the top of my body while my pulsating meat impaled him.

I placed one hand on his chest and the other on his stomach, then began to rub. Side to side, circular, up and down, my hands and fingers covered every inch of his chest, belly and arm pits with a deep, stimulating massage. As I slid one hand under his oiled cock, the fully erect organ sprang off his belly like a catapult, then returned to slam across the back of my hand. I kept it there and dug my fingers deep into the lowest part of his belly, just above his pubic hairs.

"Why do you make us do this to you? Why must we torture you?"

Deep groans reverberated from his chest, while he writhed and arched his back, further submitting himself to my worship and torment. His undulating gyrations and vise-like clinching from above thoroughly stimulated my pulsating pecker and I increased the intensity of my chest and belly rub.

"How can you endure such punishment? What more must we do to you?"

My finger found his navel and dug in deep. The muscle beneath was as hard as a brick. He arched his back even higher and sucked in his middle section to stretch his belly as tight as it could be. All the while, manly groans of pain and pleasure echoed throughout the room. Neglecting his bouncing peter, both my hands found his helplessly stretched nipples and began to pinch and twist.

Convulsions rippled from his head to his toes. He flexed his leg muscles to further stretch his body and increase the intensity of his self-imposed punishment. Inside, the innards of his rectum crushed me in their warm, undulating vise and my cock grew stronger, longer and thicker. My devastating spear tortured my helpless victim.

I whispered to him, "Talk, Nolan. Talk now. No man can take this."

The convulsive frenzy of his rectal walls finished me. My nuts were shrinking, preparing to explode, and just as they did, I took my right hand from his nipple and transferred it to his cock. Instantly, I squeezed the hell out of that thing and stroked with a savage fury. Curt's oil-slicked organ was wrenched in my hand. My fingers encircled his massive mushroom head and twisted back and forth like I was opening a jar of mayonnaise, which is exactly what I got.

Unbridled contortions of sheer orgasmic heaven shook the entire bedframe, as rapid-fire bullets of come simultaneously spattered his chest and flooded his rectum. Unholy cries from two healthy males nearly shattered the windows. Both of us flexed and tensed our interlocked bodies. Our nuts released their youthful seed in an explosive display, massive doses built from waiting, from the discovery of something new, from both pretend and very real torment. His crushing anus reduced my pecker to the diameter of a soda straw, or so it felt to me, while my frantic hand-strokes upon the full length of his penis peppered his chest and belly with hot bullets of white.

As we released the used air in our lungs and gasped for more, the strength of our eruptions faded, even though the intensity of their pleasure did not. I continued to manually stroke, which caused him to clinch his insides around me until we both collapsed in wholly satisfied exhaustion.

Then, we both laid there for the longest time, just breathing heavily and enjoying our come-down. His hands remained folded under my head, while mine wrapped around his protruding chest, holding him tightly against mine. With his constant ass-clinching now crushing a softening peter, I gently slipped out of his hole, which brought us both back to reality. "Oops," Curt chuckled. "I lost you."

"Yeah, well, you got everything out of it. I'm sure of that."

"Glad you got the towels." He grabbed one and rolled off of me and the bed, where standing revealed long lines of sticky sperm in the middle of his chest. A long, thick line of Curt's manly juice connected the pit of his stomach to his navel, where a huge puddle slowly dribbled out of its hole.

"That's a whole lotta come, Curt."

"Yeah, I think that's a topper."

"Hate to guess how much I left in you."

"What happens to it?"

"Well, I think you gotta shit it out. Speaking of shit..."

I looked down to see, thankfully, nothing but oil covering my dick. Everything had gone splendidly and I suspected to soon again visit my friend's dark hole, no longer fearful that anything disgusting would be left behind on my precious pecker.

Just then, Curt got a funny look on his face. "Uh, I think that time's about now."

He ran to the bathroom to make echoing sounds of liquid farts. While this was going on, I cleaned myself and the bed sheets, wondering if he'd still feel ok about what had just happened. Having fluids come out your ass normally is not a pleasant experience and I didn't know how he would react, but when he returned Curt was all smiles.

"Man, that was weird."

"Did it feel as good coming out as it did going in?"

"No. It's no big deal, though."

"Hey, Curt, we forgot to compare hard-ons."

"Maybe next time. I guess they're both good enough for what we wanna do."

"How 'bout a shower?"

"Definitely."

So, we did a compare and contrast with our hardened peckers under spraying water, and to our delight, the identical characteristics held true under both normal and aroused conditions. Once erect, we had no choice but to suck each other off. Curt enjoyed my services first, then he did me and we came out of the shower clean as could be.

We decided things couldn't get much better for one day, as far as excitement goes, so at about three o'clock he went home and I took a little nap. My dick was hard the entire time, but the baby oil eventually solved that problem. Amazing what the nuts could do back in those days.

Several more sleep overs took place before both of us left our parents' nest, and each one was carefully planned to give us the next morning alone to do as we pleased. We found many new discoveries with which to entertain ourselves, but once we headed off to college the games were no more.

We did get together one more time during the Christmas break. The opportunity was there for something heavy, but instead we spent most of that time talking about new friends and things we had done with them. After doing a sixty-nine with me hovering on top, we never shared an orgasm again. Memories of what we looked like, what we thought and what we did faded to fog.

I suppose my mind set has changed to the tune of 'The Thrill is Gone.' It was a great adventure and valuable learning experience, but just an early phase in my bedroom life that came and went. In fantasy all is perfect; in reality events unfold unexpectedly, the groundwork laid by dreams of what could never be. And because it is unplanned, reality is far more stimulating. If you don't believe me, read on.

ELEVATED LUST

PART ONE – WONDERFUL WEDNESDAYS

My parents were insistent that I attend college after high school, and even though I was bored with the education scene I took advantage of their good intentions to make my escape. Choosing a college in the big city, I left my small home town with no fear and no regrets, never to look back. Of course, moving to the city and functioning in the city are two different things. To say that I was naive would be right on target, but I did manage to quickly solve one problem presented to me by mom and dad.

Part of the deal was that I would have to join the labor force if I wanted to have any fun money for my personal enjoyment, for my own entertainment. Housing, food and all other expenses of necessity were paid for by mom and dad, so for myself I scouted for employment that would allow me to study while on the job. Retail seemed to be the perfect answer. Finding a department store that appeared to have very little traffic, I applied for work in the area I thought would be the slowest of all – men's dress hats, which were a gradually dying commodity.

This careful planning paid off handsomely. Rarely did I have to assist any more than ten customers during the entire shift, and since my department manager, my boss, left for home one hour after I arrived, I spent most of my time hitting the books and being paid to do so.

The highlight of this job came on Wednesdays, when the Montgomery maintenance man came to do routine checkups on their escalators and elevators. In the back of my stock room, filled with shelves of hat-containing boxes not likely to be sold was the engine room that ran the elevator, which was around the corner from my selling floor. This man, named John McMurtry, would pass through my department and into my stock room to do his weekly maintenance on the elevator motor.

He was an extremely cheerful and energetic man who always stopped to have conversations with me before going about his duties. This gave me a welcomed break from the boredom of the job and tedium of my studies.

John had led an adventurous life and enjoyed telling me of his many escapades from his Navy days where he had served during the Viet Nam War. Reliving the wild shore leaves he and his buddies had experienced, John's eyes would light up and body become animated, as he verbally and physically displayed for me his thrilling sexual encounters. When he talked about some of the Philippine bar girls he had boinked, his masterful thrusting and twisting dramatically brought his story to life, and I envisioned him nakedly performing his manly duties. This would force me to remain behind the counter in order to hide my big boner. Soon, just the sight of him would make my dick hard and I would automatically take my position of safe concealment.

In retrospect, it is perfectly understandable to me why John affected me this way, but at the time it was a puzzler. You see, when I said I was naive, my specific ignorance came from confusion in regards to my sexual inclinations. My high school exploits led my dick to pussy holes a few times and I could always make it work, even though it left me uninspired. My pre-high school exploits involved underwear-clad overnighters with male buddies that made my dick ready for something that could never happen, and these thoughts were buried. I had declared success in banishing them, but in my subconscious, those secret desires were still there whether I was willing to admit it or not. John's presence forced me to once again deal with this troubling issue.

John rather looked like a Navy guy. His height was around five feet nine inches, while his frame was stout and stocky. His bulging, furry forearms each sported anchor tattoos and his meaty hands bore permanent scars, indicating that he had indeed participated in many a bar fight. When he doubled up his fists to re-enact these altercations from the glory days, his weapons looked like they could easily take away a man's consciousness with one swing.

Put this scene together with his company uniform – dark brown trousers inflated by his heavy thighs, black steel-toe work shoes on, let's say size ten feet, feet cushioned by brightly white work socks, and khaki shirt with the three top buttons undone, scripted with that perfectly masculine name, *John* – and you can plainly imagine the problem he presented for me. Week after week I obediently stood with my crotch hidden behind the counter and listened to his magical stories of manliness. He was a talker, not a listener. I was a listener, not a talker, and once John was finished storytelling he'd head for his motor without soliciting feedback from me, while I returned to my studies unable to concentrate because of him.

I was finding it more and more difficult not to follow him into his little room just so I could watch him work, listen to him talk and fantasize about what was hidden. After all, what would be the harm? No customers ever came around in the afternoon, plus I figured if he didn't want me bothering him he'd say so. John certainly was not a man to keep quiet if something needed to be said.

So, here it was another Wednesday and I was psyched. For two months I'd built my confidence, jacking off nightly under dorm room coverings by means of his imagined physique and imagined activities with me. I fully intended to follow this man to the little secret room and let this drama play out.

When he entered my department, I greeted him as usual. "Hey, John. What's going on today?"

"Same ol' stuff, Jason," was his standard reply, with follow-up of, "How's the homework comin'?"

"Boring as hell. I'd quit this crap and get a good paying job if I had my wish, but it would break my parents' heart. After 12 years of school, I'm ready to have some fun, but there's no time." That little speech was pre-planned as a way to focus the conversation on me for a change and not him. It worked.

"You got a girlfriend?"

Dummy me. I never pre-planned anything for that question. Never expected him to go there, and I stumbled. "Uh... hmm... nope." Then, I recovered. "No time for that either."

"You oughtta go down to the bus station and get your dick sucked. I used to do it all the time. Great way to get a quickie."

John was throwing me curves left and right. I long ago had noticed that he wore a wedding ring, and with my conservatively strict upbringing all I could think about was his infidelity. Naturally, this caused me to become judge and jury, as I coaxed him to elaborate. "You mean before you were married?"

"Nope. I'd go down there any time I was horny. Still do on occasion. You know, as the years go by women don't like to get off as much as we men do."

How cool was this? Life is for learning and John was teaching me rapid fire. I had to know more. "So, where do you go at the bus station?"

"Men's room. There's glory holes all over the place. Always good service, too."

"Glory holes?"

"Sure. Between the stalls. You look through the hole... and if a guy's next door, you stick your finger in and he'll say, "come on," then you replace your finger with your dick."

This was becoming more than I could absorb. "You let men suck your dick?"

"Hell yes, son. A blow job's a blow job. As long as it feels good, who gives a shit what's at the other end? Don't let hang ups keep you from havin' a good time."

I stood quietly dumfounded and fully erect, while John went into a long diatribe about how guys on his ship would suck him off. Seems it was common practice, especially on long voyages between ports of call. When he was finished talking, he started for the stock room, but stopped at the edge of the counter and looked down at the side view of my crotch. Too bad my job forced me to wear slacks with fabric too limp to hide what was hard. But was it really too bad? John didn't have a problem with it. "Ah, ha! Just thinkin' about it's got you all revved up. Eh, Jason?"

His meaty fist lightly touched my bicep, but in my weakened state the force was enough to make me shift my feet, moving me further from the counter for undeniable exposure. "Ha... uh... yeah, John. You got my dick all excited now."

God, this was almost too easy. As he left me and headed for his engine room, I waited for my boner to subside a little, then stepped out from behind the counter to scan the area. No customers could be seen anywhere near my department, but I kept thinking of excuses not to do what I wanted to do. Apprehension, naivete and fear tempted me to talk myself out of it. A major crossroad was presented to me in my young life, a time to make a decision to either step boldly forward or to remain miserably in a shell. "Come on, Jason," I secretly motivated myself. "Are you fucking crazy? He's waiting... he wants it... NO... I might get caught... it might piss him off... he might beat the holy crap out of me... BULLSHIT! What else could he want? He's had it done before... come on come on come on, you fucking pussy... go for it." I headed back to see what the elevator man was doing.

The door was open and light on, while the metal grate protecting the engine works had been removed. John knelt down with flashlight in hand inspecting the innards of this contraption, and having heard my footsteps he looked up and smiled when I entered the little room.

"How's it look, John?"

"It's old, but workin' fine from what I can tell. What's up?"

"Nothin'. Just wanted to watch you at work."

He saw the bulge in my slacks and smiled even bigger. "Bet I know where you're headed tonight after work."

"Well, John. I'm not thinking about that right now."

He rose to his feet and for once had nothing to say. Instead, he pointed to his chest and raised one eyebrow. I nodded yes. He rubbed his crotch. I nodded yes.

"Well, shit, son. You don't have to ask me twice. Close that door and lock it."

I turned to seal us in while John unbuckled his belt. His trousers dropped to his ankles, leaving his shirt tail draped over his white boxers. Kneeling before him, I gently pulled down his undershorts until they joined his trousers, then I took his penis in hand, directing it to my waiting lips.

John left his arms hanging at his sides and surrendered his cock to me, as I slowly coaxed him with my tongue.

Ahhh... it all sounds so bliss, doesn't it? Ahhh... *I slowly coaxed him with my tongue.* What a load of crap! Being as how this was the first time my tongue had ever been anywhere near a man's penis, my tongue coaxed nothing. It was scared to death, same as I was. My tongue did nothing more than timidly lick John's spongy mushroom, fearful to go any further. Stupidly, I grabbed his shaft with my hand and tried to stroke it like I'd so many times stroked my own, but this did nothing for him. My jaw refused to open, and the meaningless tongue licks – so apprehensively delicate that my taste buds barely felt him and his penis undoubtedly felt little or nothing of me, caused John to exhale a sigh of frustration. He instantly knew that he had been duped by a first-timer.

And what did he do about it? He said, "Shit, Jason... I'll bet that concrete floor's killing your knees. Let's try something better."

The top of the motor casing was about three and a half feet high. It sat on a concrete slab with edges extended at a width sufficient for standing. As I stood to meet John eye to eye, grateful that his expression was kind and not frustrated or angry, my attention was directed to the motor casing by John's pointing thumb.

He unbuttoned his shirt, dropped it to the floor. With a wink, John waddled to the casing, his trousers and underwear at his ankles limiting the size of his steps. He made his way to the concrete ledge, stepped up one foot at a time and turned around. With elbows bent, John put his hands atop the casing and lifted himself to sit, legs dangling on either side of its corner. With another wink to motivate me, he laid back, locked his hands behind his head to use for a pillow, and waited.

Do you not think that John erased my fears? And why would he bother? Hell, he'd been sucked off countless times by world-class professionals. Why would he make himself my training ground? And in a situation that could be dangerous for both of us if caught?

I couldn't tell, but I do know that for better or worse I was going to give this man my best effort. The key word here is man. Never before had I analyzed the difference, but my fantasies always involved a man – not a young man as I was that day, but a fully-grown, fully-developed, virile, swaggering and strong man. John was all that and more.

To me he was glorious. John's chest was thick and strong with bushy dark hair covering his open arm pits, same shade as the deeply brown fur on his aforementioned forearms. His chest had a small tuft of hair in the middle and soft, silky follicles encircling his handsomely stretched nipples. With arms up and hands behind his head, his chest elevated well above his abdomen, which was stretched and declining towards me.

I stepped onto the concrete ledge at its corner for a better view. Scanning down from the end of John's sternum, his flattened belly was a sight to behold. Wide and solid as a brick wall, it seemed disproportionally long in comparison to his compact chest, almost as though this section of meat, unprotected by bone but well defended by muscle, was the focal point of his entire body. His navel was deeply inset and its oval shape nearly closed from stretching. This highlighted the pattern of fur directly below it, which began as a thin trail before widening as it approached his heavenly, golden brown and curly pubic hairs.

And there rested his waiting penis, waiting for stimulation. I took it from him, my hands never touching him. My tongue scooped beneath his corona, lifting him for my lips to embrace, and once my lips and tongue imprisoned him in their warmth and wetness, John groaned with delight, expanding his chest and sucking in his belly.

John's reaction sealed my fate. This momentous occasion was stage one of my life's dedication. Right then and there, I vowed to become a world-class cock sucker, for there is nothing more beautiful in this world than the penis of a man when it's under your control, especially when that man's penis is fully erect to fully display its incredible power. John's was fully erect in about one minute.

It is not my habit to detail dimensions of the male organs I have conquered. I prefer for you to use your imagination to make it your ideal, but because John's was my first, it is important to know that his was the perfect size for my learning. Still, I will be somewhat vague. The head of his mushroom made contact with the back of my throat at the same time my lips touched his pelvic bone. This in itself was a major milestone for me, because it comfortably taught me to repel my gagging mechanism for those over-sized monsters down the road. Specifically, John's shaft diameter fell in the range between one to one and a half inches, while his mushroom head added another half-inch. Circumcision made his corona readily available. The triangular skin formation on its underside was super-sensitive for him, a discovery my tongue quickly made and quickly exploited. My pace was probably too fast in the beginning, mostly from lack of confidence, lack of knowing what to do, but as my eyes drifted from his pubic hairs, to his belly button, to his stomach, to his chest, armpits and close-eyed serene face, my concentration shifted from the seemingly unnatural sensation of cock in my mouth to the perfectly masculine man to whom it belonged. I slowed everything down, just so I could enjoy John's beautiful torso.

This worked for him, I think. He gave no indication as to my effectiveness – no sounds, no words, no physical writhing or undulations. John laid quietly with eyes closed and just a hint of grin, corners of his mouth lifted ever so slightly. My service upon him warranted no more and no less, just a basic gliding down to the base and back to the head, my tongue comfortably but not tightly wrapped around his underside. My first true test came when somebody out in the department store needed the elevator. With button pushed, the aging motor directly beneath us came to life with a loud click and mighty whoosh. John was used to it, but not I, and it is a miracle that my teeth didn't tear him to pieces. While the rest of me nearly jumped out of my shoes, somehow my mouth froze in place with tongue and roof of mouth protecting him until I calmly resumed my stroking.

Everything turned out ideally for me. My first time cock sucking technique was average at best, and so John's volume of semen was mediocre at best, something I could not have judged at the time. What he gave me was easily swallowed. He never warned me verbally or physically that he was coming. This is also just as well, for had I known that John was coming it is likely I would have panicked and gagged, or worse, spit out his cock as he tried to fire, which is good reason for a cock sucker to receive an angry fist.

John was courteous as he rose from his prone position. He thanked me, hoping I would not solicit a grade from him. I thanked him, hoping but doubting that he would ever again allow me to waste his time.

As I handed him his shirt John said, "Damn, Jason. I don't know if I can wait for next Wednesday."

"Really? Oh... uh... yeah, me neither."

"Got a phone number?"

"Sure do. Here and home. Want me to write them down for you?"

"Yep."

PART TWO – THE WILD SIDE OF LIFE

I thought the nine o'clock closing would never arrive. Lifted to a natural high, I was totally consumed by the masculine marvel I had just serviced. I couldn't concentrate on my studies, so I closed the books and just stood there behind the counter, dreamily gazing into nothingness. Couldn't wait to get back to the dorm so I could jack off, so I didn't. John's little motor room was just as good for singles as for pairs.

Thursday came and passed – no messages for me at the dorm; no phone calls while at work. I wondered how long I'd have to worry about the truthfulness of what he'd said. John said he couldn't wait until Wednesday, and mercifully he kept his word.

Friday night, 30 minutes before closing, the phone rang. "Wilbert's Department Store, Men's Hat Department, this is Jason."

"Hello, Jason. John speakin'."

"Hey! What's up?"

"Wanna meet me somewhere tonight?"

"Sure."

"Come to Pete's Tavern on Chelsea Street. You know where that is?"

"Chelsea and what?"

"Eighteenth. 1824 Chelsea."

I was not familiar with many areas of the city, but I did know that this was on the fringes of downtown, kind of a wasteland at night, and I felt a little uneasy. "Uh, John. I'm only 19. I can't go into a bar."

"Sure you can. It's just a little neighborhood place. We all know each other. I'll take you under wing as soon as you come in and it'll be ok. I'll be there at ten and watch for you."

I had seen his solid body and menacing fists. I had seen him re-enact his many scrapes from his Navy days, so I knew he could take care of both me and himself. "Sounds good. I'll see you there."

After work I rushed to the dorm for wardrobe change. Blue jeans and pocket tee shirt on me were matched by another set placed into an overnight bag, along with fresh socks and underwear plus a few other goodies. Optimism ran high and I would not go unprepared. Jumping into the car I'd owned since I turned 16, I headed downtown, turning off of 18th onto Chelsea. My heart dropped a beat when I saw but one building with lights. Most of the buildings on this block had been torn down and the desolation combined with darkness hinted of danger. That one building, brightly lit by neon sign of blue and red identified my destination, Pete's Tavern. Attached to the end of a seemingly otherwise abandoned building, Pete's was framed on the other side by a trash strewn alley, then another empty structure. I made a U-turn and parked on the Pete side past the alley.

As soon as I entered the tiny bar a booming voice rang out. "There you are, buddy! Come over here and I'll buy you a drink."

John was bellied up to the short end of an L-shaped bar with his elbow resting on top, beer bottle in hand. He looked casually comfortable in black trousers and short-sleeved, burgundy knit shirt, the neck of which was cut in a V with three buttons. None were buttoned. The collar seemed wrinkled, while the tail hanging out was probably a little too short, but the snug fit highlighted his stocky chest, handsome biceps and tapered abdomen. Here was the unsophisticated blue-collar man, out for a friendly round of beers and conversation, ready to celebrate the weekend. I smiled and headed for him.

For a Friday night, the place was pretty quiet. Besides John, the only occupant was a half-asleep (or drunk) elderly man sitting on a stool centered at the long section of the L. Beyond that was a pool table, where three husky men were shooting for beers. A television was mounted on the wall above the bar, broadcasting some sports program about the life of boxer Roberto Duran. This definitely was a neighborhood tavern. Unfortunately, the neighborhood was dead.

John wrapped his thick arm around my shoulder and whispered. "You want me to use your real name?"

I shrugged and nodded yes, so John introduced me to the bartender. "Jack, this here's my brother's son, Jason."

Jack held out his hand. "Hello, Jason. Your uncle sure is a pain in the ass."

Gosh, I sure wanted to say something comical, you know, regarding my ass, but I played it straight as I shook the burly man's hand. "Yeah, I know. He's been pretty good to me, though, so we just put up with him."

"What'll you have there, pal? John's buyin'. "

"How about a beer? Busch or Bud. Hey! Is that Rubber Toe on the TV?" Only people who know boxing ever call him that. I figured this would earn me some brownie points.

"Yep. Hands of Steel. Busch comin' up."

John removed his arm, knowing I now felt comfortable. "Were you busy tonight?"

"Hell, no. That place is never busy. Got a lot of reading done, though."

As Jack set my bottle of Busch on the counter, John gave me a barrage of questions. For the first time since we'd met he actually wanted to know about my life, which really didn't take too long to tell. He shook his head when I explained why I was in school and how I really wasn't in the right frame of mind for it.

"Hell, Jason. You're young. You can always go to school later. If you wanna live a little first, tell you parents…"

"Hey, John!" We were rudely interrupted by one of the pool players. " Who's this little pecker head?"

John slammed his bottle onto the counter. "What's it to ya, ass wipe?"

The intruder left the table and headed our way. As he approached, his massive girth seemed to become even more intimidating. "Doesn't matter to me. I just don't think Jack likes havin' pecker heads in his bar."

My protector looked at me. "Don't worry 'bout him. He's nothin'. He's just pissed 'cause I whipped their ass at pool the other night. They bought me beers for hours, until I finally got bored embarrassin' the three of 'em."

The behemoth kept coming towards us, still talking. "Hey, John, does your little pecker head buddy play pool? Maybe he'd like to get a free beer. How 'bout it, pecker head? You wanna shoot?"

Using me to get under John's skin was this man's goal. His repeatedly calling me pecker head, however, kind of set me off.

I shouldn't have said it, but I suppose the atmosphere of the place put me in a smart ass frame of mind, so my answer to him was, "I guess if I had a choice, I'd rather be a pecker head than a pussy hole. Is that what you are, pal? A pussy hole?"

The shit was on. He lunged for me and I quickly shifted to one side, while John stepped up to greet him with a left jab to the sternum that stopped him dead in his tracks and gasping for air.

"Hold it right there, Charlie," John warned him. "Don't be fuckin' with us."

As the other two came over to rescue their pal, Jack the bartender barked at us all. "That's enough fellas. None of this shit in my bar. You know the rules. Take it outside... NOW!"

John and Charlie stood toe to toe with their chests puffed up and fists clenched while staring each other down. The brute was a full head taller and several inches wider than my partner, but John was unfazed, fully prepared to take on this hulk with no fear whatsoever. My protector waved me towards the door. "C'mon nephew, let's leave these boys to their precious pool game. They aren't worth fuckin' with." He took a step back and queried the bartender. "Jack, are the beers covered?"

"Yeah, John. There's more than enough here." He took what he needed for the beers and came around the bar, stuffing the rest into John's pocket. "Charlie, back off. John here's responsible for this kid, so you just fix your problem some other time."

I waited by the door while John headed my way, walking backwards and keeping an eye on the three aggressors. Once there we both exited to the sidewalk, and then John grabbed me by the arm, dragging me into the alley where we stood side by side with him closer to the corner of the building. "Watch this, Jason. These dummies are gonna come after us."

Under normal circumstances, I should have been pissed at him. Why would he bring me to this forsaken part of town? He obviously knew it was likely we'd end up in an altercation. And all of this was happening on our first "date" outside the department store. But how could I be angry with John? Hell, I needed him for my survival. I certainly was not going to start bitching at him now.

Truth be known exhilaration best describes what I felt. The sight of this man, my buddy John, as he boyishly grinned while breathing heavily from his excitement of the battle to come, thrilled me no end. He wanted me to become witness and participant to his wild side, perhaps to show me that all his talk in the department store wasn't just a load of hot air. We were like youngsters playing cops and robbers, with him being the sheriff and me his deputy. I could think of no better place to be than by his side as we crouched in waiting for the bad guys.

Sure enough, we heard the door open and men talking. "Where'd they go, Charlie?"

"I don't know. Hey! That's gotta be the kid's car. Let's trash it. That'll flush 'em out."

As Charlie stepped towards my car and cleared the corner of the building, John pounced on him. He clamped on a headlock, extended his hip and flipped Charlie onto the sidewalk flat on his back. Immediately, the other two came at John from behind. One grabbed his arms and held them back, while the other moved in front and began punching John's belly. One blow after another landed with a deep thud, as John tensed those strong muscles to receive their punishment as though they had no effect on him whatsoever.

But they did have an effect. It doesn't matter how strong a man is, sooner or later unrestricted punches to his gut will break down that wall, and once that happens everything inside becomes vulnerable to rupture. I had no clue as to what John planned to do about this, but I did know that I sure as hell wasn't going to stand there and watch it happen.

What John didn't know, and what those three men didn't know, was that Roberto Duran had nothing on me. That is a gross exaggeration, but my good buddy from my little home town had a father who at one time had been a semi-professional boxer, and when we were kids this man devoted many hours to showing us the skills necessary for situations just like this. John was outnumbered. I reacted.

Stepping to my right from around the corner, I surprised the man holding John's arms and delivered a left hook directly to his rib cage, sending him into a backwards and sideways stagger. He tripped over his own feet, bouncing the back of his head on concrete and sounding like a bowling ball as the impact of noggin to sidewalk efficiently knocked him out. Meanwhile, John unleashed a furious assault on the fellow in front of him. Punch after punch pounded the man on his face, chest, belly and any other body parts that happened to get in John's way. John was like a hurricane. I stood in awe of his speed and power. John's attack was savage, intimidating, and a major turn-on for me. My little sparkplug overwhelmed the much bigger man, pulverizing him into a blathering idiot.

Unbeknownst to me, Charlie had regained his feet and moved into the alley behind me. He tapped me on the shoulder and I turned to see a looping, roundhouse right headed my way. Obviously, this man knew nothing about boxing, because his swing was so wide and so slow that I easily avoided it by stepping to my right. With feet firmly planted, I shot a left hook to the side of his belly followed by a right cross landing squarely on his ear, made readily available to me by Charlie's bending forward from my shot to his gut, and if you've never been hit on your ear there's no way for me to tell you how bad it hurts.

I heard crackling sounds and was unsure whether it was my knuckles or his cartilage that had been smashed, but as Charlie fell first to his knees and then to his face, a trickling line of blood exited his ear hole, telling me my right hand had scored a direct hit. I figured Charlie would be giving us no more trouble for quite some time.

John had totally subdued the other guy with his barrage of blows, which now included kicks as well as punches. The poor fellow was curled into a ball down on the sidewalk and covering his head with both arms, begging for John to stop beating him. And the funniest part of this is that while John savagely brutalized his man, he ignored his man. Instead, he enjoyed the scene in the alley way as Charlie tumbled face-first to asphalt. How's that for domination?

Meanwhile, the third man had apparently awakened less courageous than before I'd sucker-punched him, because he ran for his pickup truck, squealing tires to make his quick get-away.

I looked at John and he at me, then we both cracked up. The John-battered man saw his chance to escape and did so by running down the street, leaving poor Charlie to fend for himself. So much for loyalty. John approached the big man, who was still laying on the alley asphalt, rubbing the side of his head and smearing blood from ear to his cheek.

John taunted him. "What's wrong with you, tough guy?"

Charlie rolled onto his back and raised himself to sit. "Wha... what the hell happened?" The fall onto his face seemed to have bloodied his nose, too, but that wasn't my fault. He should have taken his hands off of his gut to break his fall.

John turned to me with another of those friendly fists to the bicep. "Did you do this to him? You big bully."

I beamed with pride while John continued to torment poor Charlie. "Look here, asshole. Next time you see me and my buddy here, you better head for the hills. This here is OUR bar and OUR pool table. Don't you let us catch you around here again, or we will whip your ass three times worse than we did tonight. Got it?"

Charlie nodded his head in the affirmative, then struggled to his feet and headed towards his car. We watched and waved as he drove away at a rapid pace, running the corner stop sign and ignoring his unfaithful, frantically waving companion.

"C'mon, Jason. How about another beer?"

"Sounds good to me."

John expertly relayed the recent events to Jack the bartender, while the old man remained passed out on his same stool. I watched and listened as John talked a mile a minute, punctuating his story with the punches he and I had thrown. As for Jack, he didn't seem overly impressed with any of this, leading me to believe that John's exploits were a rather common occurrence, but when the demise of Charlie was retold Jack interrupted.

"Wait a minute. You mean the kid downed him?"

John's eyes grew even wider. "Sure as hell did... and fast, too."

"I don't believe it. Show me, Jason."

All of a sudden, I was the big talker retelling my tale. I was the one expertly acting out each punch with a dramatic flair to rival John's.

Now, not only was Jack interested, he was more than impressed. He stood wide-eyed with mouth agape as I maneuvered through my accurate displays of boxing techniques.

"God damn, John. You better not piss this guy off," Jack warned. "I bet he could take you in a heartbeat."

John wrapped his arm around me and gave a mighty squeeze. "We'll never know, Jack, 'cause it ain't ever gonna happen."

Needless to say, I was feeling very important. I had just been initiated into a most special fraternity – an honored member of the secret society of accomplished bar room brawlers. Even though I didn't look or feel the part, I was proud to have been accepted and couldn't wait to see how John and I would celebrate this glorious occasion.

After another beer we returned to the street.

"Is that your car, Jason?"

"Yep."

"Follow me. I got a reward for you... my knight in shining armor, comin' to my rescue."

Staying close behind John's big Mercury, I trailed him into the parking garage of the Cloverleaf Hotel, a seedy looking place in a downtown building. Soon we were in an eighth floor room complete with one full-size bed, one bedside table, one lamp, one white-washed window, one mirror on a side wall, one sink, one toilet and one stand-up shower stall.

I dropped my bag on the floor and John was glad to see it. "Come prepared, did ya?"

"Yep."

"You wanna shower first, or should we go at it all hot and sweaty?"

"What say we do hot and sweaty first, then clean and sweet-smellin' later?"

"Sounds like a plan, Jason."

PART THREE – MY SAILOR

We stripped. I was faster because I was horny, plus I wanted to watch him undress and did so by seizing the middle of the bed. I laid chest up on top of the covers, head on pillows. First item? John's shirt. He lifted it over his head, carelessly dropping it to the floor. Grabbing his belt strap, he violently yanked to release its prong from his chosen hole, and for a flashing second he sucked in his belly to ease the tightening of his belt. This move, along with all that followed was done with his usual bravado. John oozed machismo. He couldn't help himself.

He sat on the bed. Meticulously, he one at a time untied his shoe laces and slipped off his shoes and socks, hand-wiping the soles of his feet upon exposure. Standing and turning to again face me, he dropped his trousers, stepping out of them but leaving enough fabric draped over one instep to deftly lift his trousers from foot to hand. John shook out the wrinkles, and then sloppily half-folded before stacking his trousers atop his shoes and socks. On top of that he laid his shirt. Last item? John's boxer shorts. He nonchalantly tucked his thumbs beneath their waistband, lowered them to his thighs and let gravity do the rest. His pile was complete and he stood with both corners of lips upturned, alternating his eyes between me on the bed and my bag on the floor.

"You're the man, John," I instructed him. "Explore my bag, get what you want and be a man."

Our conversation was over. He looked inside and found what I knew would make him happy – a jar of petroleum jelly. I later learned that baby oil would have made him even more happy, but again John silently forgave me for my inexperience.

After retrieving a hand towel from the tiny bathroom he joined me on the bed, coaxing me to roll onto my belly. Next, he guided me to an all-fours position on hands and knees. After my ass rim was thoroughly jellied, John lubricated his penis, confirmed for me by the squishing sounds of jelly between fingers, corona and shaft. John stroked until hard. He pressed his helmet against the rim of my ass, and immediately my natural reflexes clinched in defense.

John backed away. He wrapped the arm of his dry left hand around my belly, gently rubbing with his scratchy palm. His lips touched my lower back, while a finger pressed against my ass. He forcefully exhaled, purposely, allowing his warm, manly breath to comfort me. John's hard-skinned palm and beer-tainted breath did comfort me, but not nearly so much as John's patience with me. He could have rudely plowed his way in and forced me to accept it, but like I said, John oozed machismo and he treated me as a man on equal terms with him, not as some meaningless come tank given to his pleasure.

Penetration of one finger was painless, but tight. He waited a few seconds before inserting a second finger to join the first, taking both into me inches at a time until his knuckles pressed my butt cheeks. Withdrawing, he slow stroked with two, added a third and loosened my vise. Kisses and hot breath to my back combined with hand-rubs to my belly did the trick. I was ready for John.

His mushroom entered and John allowed its swollen head to linger near the inside of my rectal hole. How many times had I watched his re-enactments? His countless air fucks of unknown Philippine girls? My curiosities and longings for what a man like John could do to me would soon be known.

Slowly, he delved deeper, left hand still on my belly, right hand now on my right shoulder. Along my spine he pecked me with kisses, on both my butt cheeks he tickled with his pubic hairs, and without my knowledge he conquered me. John was mine and I was his, his penis into me as deep as he could go. Now as artists we created.

Placing his hands into my arm pits, John lifted me to stand on my knees, all the while keeping his cock buried deep into my hole. He took my wrists and raised them over our heads, placing my hands to the back of his head. Releasing them, John left my hands for me to clamp onto him, and as I ran my fingers through his hair, half-dry and half-damp with sweat, John ran the palms of his hands up and down the length of my wide open chest and belly. Rough, scratchy, working-man hands built from labor, hardened from fist fights, John's leathered palms toughened me, made me forget about his impaling thick cock, made me reach further back with my hands to stretch my chest and belly for his gentle abuse.

"Look, Jason."

I turned my head to the right. In the side wall mirror our side view reflection was perfectly framed, John's knees inside of mine, John's thighs, hips and buttocks flexing in calm exertion. Had he planned this? Did he wish to prove that his boastful re-enactments were genuine in reality? I could see him. I could feel him. I could be witness to a master at work, and my hard dick surged to new strength.

John planted both hands firmly onto my chest and buried his lips into the meat of my right trapezius. His hot exhale of breath warmed my right pectoral, no longer the breath of a man but of a mighty bull preparing to charge forward. He slowly moved his cock back towards my rim, then swivelled his hips to thrust at me from a different angle. His strokes were methodical and magical, each time coming from a new height, inches to the left or right. He established no pattern. I never knew from which direction he would come next despite my watching him in the mirror. With my eyes transfixed on him, what I saw is all I needed to know. John's compact and powerful body twisted, flexed and undulated towards me and away from me.

This beautiful man overwhelmed me with his masculine dominance. New layers of sweat lubricated the skin of his chest and belly, squishing between us as he danced his magical ballet of intercourse. His manly grace juxtaposed with his dominating strength. John danced for me, but with conviction. He led and I followed, as his masterful, hip-swivelling, forward-thrusting cock retracted and recoiled to return and stir my innards from every possible angle.

With powerful hands pressing deeply all areas of my chest and belly, John's anchor tattoos came to life. Their dark green ink took on a brightened sheen. His forearms glistened with sweat. His tattoos rippled and rolled, as the muscles and ligaments of his forearms strained and flexed, guiding his organ of impalement to and fro, up and down, left and right.

Suddenly, John was my Navy man. I tousled his hair to complete my image, toughening him, making him appear more rugged than he already was. He womanized me. Miles from nowhere on the vast ocean, this masculine sailor had chosen me for breeding. His hot breath melted my neck. His manly sweat lathered my back. His powerfully skilled cock rendered me an accepting rag.

Transformed from ignorant virgin to mesmerized know-it-all, I timed my squeezing to coincide with his dominating thrusts. My desire was to bring him a pleasured insanity, so I brutally crushed his massive organ upon its deepest penetration. My hands frantically massaged his scalp and neck. I extended the full length of my arms to lovingly coax him towards orgasmic heaven.

With my participation spurring him, John's tempo intensified. My muscled innards locked him in their vise, desperately trying to keep him inside me forever. I wanted his seed. I demanded his seed, and John's increasingly labored breathing, thrusting and flexing hinted that his time was near.

But just when I thought our ecstatically combined utopia could reach no higher level, this precious man further elevated me. He reached forward with his right hand. He clasped his rough, working-man's palm around the shaft of my cock and stroked me with his thick fingers.

I nearly cried out, but it had nothing to do with scratchy fingers.

What kind of man was this? There was no need for him to stroke me, but his reflected image proved what I felt. I fought to control my emotions. I bit my tongue to prevent its speaking words that could ruin everything – those three words from which meaningful sex constricts to unwanted peripherals. I never dreamed that John could be such a man. I was no Philippine girl to him. He could have fucked me, put on his clothes and gone on home. But no. He wanted me to get off, too. Some tough guy he turned out to be. How could I have known that he was just as beautiful on the inside as on the outside? Hell, I would have been satisfied with the outside alone, but that wasn't good enough for him. This man, this rugged, purely masculine and macho tough guy wanted me to get off with him. I turned away from the mirror. He would not see my tears. Who did he think he was making me feel this way?

As John fought my anal vise, his mouth clamped onto the meat of my shoulder. A love bite it was, a display of domination, a controlling chomp to keep me steady while flooding me with his seed. He forcefully withdrew his cock and speared me with a return thrust, nearly driving his powerful pole into my belly while firing his second burst of come. And as John filled my bowels, his stroking hand coaxed my own explosion, its initial volley arcing gracefully to splatter the cheap wood of our headboard.

I was too weak, bordering on unconsciousness, but John held me up, one hand on my chest and the other on my cock, while frantically stroking me by his hand and his dick. Two male organs contracted to spew. With my eyes closed, all remembered images of John combined with real-time sensations of John finished me. John alone finished us both.

As his body relaxed, John rested his head on my shoulder. He let go my spent penis and resumed hugging my belly. For our come-down, John steadied himself and me, his powerful rod slowly losing its strength inside me. I courageously returned to our mirrored image, my hands still clamped to the back of his head, his face pressed to my deltoid. Nothing was spoiled. John's dormant body was just as beautiful as the active – even more so now that it was over, now that his masterful penis had ingested me with his toughness, with his "don't give a shit" attitude, with his kind-hearted patience and acceptance of me.

Size shrinkage let him slip out. No John bravado for this, no pain for me. I immediately turned to tell him what I thought, but John collapsed backwards onto the bed, chest up and arms hanging off the end of the mattress. Guess he didn't need to hear what he already knew. At least I'd found a way to keep him from talking for awhile.

Instead of talking, he was snoring. Poor thing. He was so exhausted, and so beautiful. Drenched in sweat, chest heaving, belly majestically rising and falling, John's naked body laid right there wide open and at my disposal. But you've got to understand something. I didn't know the rules. That probably doesn't make any sense now. After all, he'd already been in my mouth and my ass, but this wasn't just a couple of giddy youngsters playing around. This was the real deal. This was a real man, and I didn't know how much leeway I was going to be given when it came down to what I could touch and what I could not.

Still naive, I saw John as a straight fellow who was just being nice to me. I hadn't quite figured it all out yet, but I gathered my courage – the courage given to me by him, laid down on my side and rested with my elbow near his rib cage. I gently put my hand to his sternum, and in a flash John sprang up with both fists clenched and ready to fly before recognizing where he was and who was touching him.

"Shit, Jason. You startled me. Be careful about that. I don't want to punch you out." He laid back down and closed his eyes.

After my heart slowed down a bit, I analyzed what had just happened and came to the conclusion that I'd better keep my hands off. I figured he could sleep while I showered, but as I rummaged through my bag for necessities John opened his eyes.

"What are you doing, Jason?"

"Thought I'd get cleaned up."

"You know, those fellas beat on me pretty good."

"I know, John. I'm sorry. I should have jumped in sooner."

"Nah, nah... I didn't mean that. Hell, you saved my ass, Jason. I'll never forget it. What I mean is that I'm pretty sore. Sure could use a rub."

Dropping everything, I laid right back where I had been on the same elbow. My hand massaged his chest, palm running atop each pectoral. "How's that?"

"Nuh." Bland response tinted with disgust, John was unimpressed, so I moved to where I knew they'd punched him, his stomach and belly.

"There?"

"Come on, Jason. Get up on your hands and knees. Work me over good and deep."

In other words, be a man, use your man's strength. I knelt beside him, grabbed his spongy peter and brushed it aside towards his balls, and then with fingertips dug into hard, sore muscle.

"Ah, yeah... that's more like it. Let me stretch 'em out a bit."

He brought his hands together beyond his head and angled them straight-armed towards the floor. His chest rose up, belly sank down, abdominals tightened. Like an elongated, vulnerable mass of dough, John's middle section succumbed to my manipulating fingers. Digits encircled his navel, impaling and kneading relaxed but solid muscle. John let me in. As his built-up tension lessened, my fingers dug deeper, my right hand working on his belly, left on his stomach.

"There's a sore spot on my right... a little more... that's it. Do it."

I gladly did it until his tightness disappeared, leaving his natural toughness restored. From here, all middle section was deep-rubbed and manipulated, everywhere from his rib cage to pelvic bone, all meat unprotected by bone. And when his tight spots were obliterated, John's belly received heated friction by way of my palms performing a frantic side to side massage.

"Ah, that's good stuff. Those mother fuckers hit me all over, huh, Jason?"

"Yep. They got you good."

He raised his head, bringing his arms back onto the mattress in a crucifixion sprawl. "Damn, Jason. You really like men, don't you."

John stared at my dick with eyes bright and teeth showing. Erections never lie. "Hey, John, I like you. That's all I know. Got any more sore spots?"

"Maybe." He grinned before dropping his head. "Let me shower and we'll find out."

"Don't you dare."

"Well, fuck you then... I'll stay here."

"How about these? Are they sore?" I started with his hands, as he laid with arms perpendicular to his body and palms up.

"Yeah... mm hm... they could use some work." I was already thumb-massaging his right hand and squeezing his fingers when he answered me. After leaping across his chest I got his left hand, too. Then I kissed it, scratched my face for good measure.

"I'll bet this hurts," I guessed in reference to his forearm.

"Oh, sure... why not."

From here on out, most of my massaging was done by lips and tongue with a few fingers and palms occasionally added for variety. That anchor tattoo had to be kissed and licked. The hairs of his arms had to tickle my face. Another leap over him brought me to his right arm for a repeat dose of praise.

"This has got to be in bad shape," I said before moving my tongue from muscular bicep to bushy arm pit.

"It's gotta be funky. I guarantee you that."

"Won't be when I'm finished. It'll smell like my spit." I tossed his arm beyond his head, elbow to hand hanging off the mattress. My tongue and lips saturated with no inhibitions. John's funk was inhaled, spat upon and licked, as I explored the smell and taste of a real man. "Like that?"

"Hell, yes."

"Good, then I'll do the other one, too."

For my interest, I exited the bed and grabbed his left wrist, stretching his arm towards me. Wide open, his left arm pit got the same treatment from above, and when I was finished his arms were exactly how I needed them to be – sprawled past his head off the mattress and angled towards the floor by gravity.

"Now, here's a curiosity," I observed while kneeling next to his expanded and elevated rib cage. "Does this work for you?" My lips encircled his handsomely stretched tit.

"Uh... I don't know. Why don't you show me?"

I already was. I worked on my technique, discovering that sucking around his diameter while licking his tip caused a disturbance down below. John's nut-resting penis swelled just a bit.

"I seem to be getting something here, John. I better try the other one."

John raised his head to confirm what he felt. "I'll be damned. There is something going on." With head on the mattress and eyes closed, John raised his chest to stretch his tits a little more, as I tongue-wet the dry one and finger-pinched the wet one. Now, I was the teacher. Losing himself in something new, John's cock grew strong enough to raise off of his nuts and nestle between his thigh and belly. "Man, oh man, Jason. All this time... got a hot spot I didn't even know about."

This made me wonder what else he didn't know. Learning that John wasn't such an expert on everything elevated me to a level nearer to him, but I still had a long way to go. I would make John my classroom and he would let me.

"Hey, John. What size feet are those?"

"Nines."

"Nines? How the hell do you stay standing?"

"Got strong toes, I guess."

"I guess," as I sucked on a great one. He bent all five back when I licked on his arch, accommodating me as I touched, tasted and smelled hard-skinned, working-man feet. By the time I'd finished with his other foot John's firm dick had shifted again, now pointing more to his belly button.

"You've sure got hairy legs."

"Sorry."

"Don't be." Like everywhere else I'd been, John's body hairs were made darker with my painting tongue, his dried sweat replaced by my spit. Both shins, both calves, both knees and both thighs, I spared nothing until reaching his golden V where two delectable balls lay waiting.

"What the hell are you... a man or a bull?"

"Just a dog, Jason. That's all I am." And just as a dog does when sunning his belly in afternoon rays, John drew up his knees and spread his legs into a butterfly. His nuts were fully exposed.

Here is where my master's thesis was written, for here is where a man is won or lost. His gonads, so sensitive, require great skill to properly stimulate without threatening discomfort, but once conquered, the man is completely under your control. From then on, you can do just about whatever you want to do with him.

I took my time learning how to love John's nuts. I practiced with my fingertips, delicately scratching, pinching and twisting. I tested with my lips, gently kissing, pinching and tugging on testicle hairs. I scored high marks with my tongue, slavishly flicking and licking, and by the time I'd graduated this course John's penis was frantically bouncing on his belly in an erotic ballet of syrup-oozing delight. By the time I was finished with what I needed to know, John had nothing more to say other than mesmerized groans of happiness and pitiful moans of wanting me to finish him.

"Well, John, you know that I'm certainly no expert on the matter, but god damn, that dick of yours sure is handsome."

"Um hm... mmm."

That was not much of an answer, but the good new is that because John had so recently shot me full of his semen, I was allowed plenty of time to improve my sucking skills.

"Give me that beautiful son of a bitch," I demanded upon snatching his cock with my lips. My first move was to engulf the entire thing to get it nice and wet. From there, I trained myself. Experimentations were graded by tones of voice. John's grunts, moans and groans, high-pitched, low-pitched, medium-pitched, told me what worked and how well. Such a generous teacher was John that he suffered countless near-orgasms while I filled my head with knowledge. I did eventually catch on as to how I was torturing him. I came to the realization that when he tensed up and his balls shrunk to peanuts it was rather cruel of me to change tactics and try a new technique. Bad timing? Perhaps, but even after I knew what I was doing I kept doing it because I now had good reason. John was no longer in control. I was. This was my classroom; John my guinea pig.

When I finally let John blow his load, this hard-assed tough guy whimpered like a baby. But I will say that for a man 40-something years old, his second coming that came an hour after his first was quite impressive. That was thanks to me, by my way of thinking, by my way of doing. My hour with a surrendered John taught me how to properly stimulate every body part necessary for good orgasm. I'd also made great strides in becoming what I vowed to be – a professional cock sucker. And it was only my second try!

That's all John wanted from me. He wanted me to be my best – for myself, and for him.

As I laid John's fading cock onto his belly, his snoring served as my reward. My sailor, my tough guy, expressed his gratitude by his total comfort with me, so relaxed that he dared to sleep sprawled naked with me kneeling between his thighs. Didn't he know that I might start all over on him? Torment him for another hour? Didn't he care? Probably not. John was a purely sexual man, fully confident in himself and not caring who did what as long as they did it right. Me? I intended to lick, kiss and suck to my heart's content, but with my tongue inches from his belly John awakened himself with his own snoring and rose to sit.

"I sure could use a shower to recharge my batteries. Mind if I go first?"

"Ok, go ahead... no wait... I think... feels like I need to use the bathroom."

"That's right, Jason. Might as well just say it. Think you've got diarrhea? Well, don't have a heart attack when my juice comes out your ass."

Just another well-prepared lesson for me. Thanks to John's warning, those liquid farts brought me laughter rather than alarm. I was proud to see his come floating in toilet water.

PART FOUR – NAVEL EXCHANGE

The John coming out of the shower didn't appear too much different from the John going in. This man was tired, in need of some serious sleep. As for me, I toyed with the idea of jacking myself while he cleaned up, but managed to keep my hands off just in case John had other plans after his nap. I shouldn't have been concerned. In those days I could get off anytime I wanted, but with a man like John in my midst, I figured denying myself would heighten my enthusiasm for whatever else he wanted to do with me.

I was a little reluctant to shower. Somehow I wanted to keep for a little while longer the odors attached to me. On various parts of my skin I could smell John, the sailor man and bar room brawler. I could smell Pete's Tavern, beer, and the men John and I as a team had manhandled. I was fearful that with the washing away of these aromas the memories would begin to fade, which was something I did not want to happen.

No need for concern. The smell of John stayed with me. It permeated my nostrils. The aromas of his body hairs were transferred to my nose hairs, and each inhale reminded me of him for days to come.

Once under the water I lingered there, halfway hoping he might join me even though space was limited. Finally, I gave up and finished lathering, rinsing and drying myself, returning to the bed where John snoozed under covers on the far side. He laid on his back, sheet draped over the end of his rib cage, head on pillow with one hand tucked beneath his head, but my naked sitting on the bed awakened him.

"Finished?"

"Yeah."

"Come on." He patted his chest, inviting me to use him for my pillow.

With my head in the crook of his arm pit, John wrapped his right arm around me and stroked my shoulder with his scratchy thumb. I stroked him too, using my right hand fingers to brush his sternum hairs while my thumb glided over his nipple.

"You feel good, Jason. Smell good, too."

"So do you."

"I shouldn't have had you meet me at that bar. Those guys usually don't come in on the weekends, so I didn't figure on seein' 'em."

"It's ok. I got a kick out of it."

"Pussies... trying to gang up on us. They sure weren't expecting you to give 'em any trouble... were they, Jason?"

"No. Had a little surprise coming."

"Surprised me, too. Where'd you learn to fight like that?"

"A friend of mine in high school showed me how to box. We used to spar all the time, but I'd never used it for real... not until tonight. Guess it worked, huh?"

John chuckled. "A sight to behold, watchin' that big dummy fall like an oak tree. One of the funniest things I've ever seen. There's a lesson for you, Jason. Just because a fella's big doesn't mean he's tough. Usually all talk... think they can intimidate you, but they can't fight a lick."

"You took care of your end, too. I thought those gut punches might get to you, but you acted like you didn't even feel 'em."

"Nah, my job keeps me pretty tight. I'm a cheater, Jason. I'll come at 'em with anything and everything, fists, feet... hell, I'll use my teeth if I have to... I ain't ever been whipped yet."

"Whatever works. You were like a buzz saw. Like a blur."

"And you were like a surgeon... a precision of incision. Hey, next time we'll just come straight here. I won't get you into a dangerous situation like that."

"What are you talking about? That was cool as hell." His nipple was pecked with my hard kiss. "Hey, man, I like hanging with you. I don't care what we're doing. I will never forget it. We're a team now... nobody can take us."

John lifted his head to kiss the crown of mine. "You're something else. How 'bout you turn off that lamp and we'll sleep awhile. Ok?"

Nestled on my sailor's chest, safe and content, I quickly fell into slumber. How, why or when I came to be using his belly for my pillow instead of his pectoral I don't know, but that's where I was upon awakening. Under covers I laid with my belly between his knees, my feet past the end of the mattress still covered by sheet and blanket, and my chest covering his penis. John snored in darkness, unfazed by the weight of my head pressing into his hard abdominals. My maneuvering had brought the covers with me, exposing him, and with no concern with waking him I kissed and licked his middle section. This time, no brine, no sweat, John smelled of soap. His skin was soft, the muscle beneath it solid. With my touch came a moment of silence, as John's snoring stopped. A pleasured "mmm" was accompanied by a wake-up stretch. John threw his arms towards the headboard and arched his back, and with circulation jump-started he slid both hands under the pillows, spreading his arms in a flat-on-mattress V pointing towards each corner. John made himself available, chest up, belly flat, as I went to work.

My suspicions about him were true. John's abdomen, exceedingly long in comparison to his chest, was a major flashpoint for him, and having my face buried there was a major turn-on for both of us. My arm threw back the covers, casting all of him in the pale grey of city lights filtered through white-painted window.

Such a contrast was this mass of middle, soft and cushioned at its surface, but an unmovable wall beneath. With deeply pressed nose and face I inhaled his strength, but I wanted more. John took my cue upon feeling my fingers under his flanks. He arched the small of his back so I could slide my hands underneath him. He tightened his muscles when I trapped his belly between my arms and my face, and when my explorations brought me to his navel, John exhaled forcefully, dramatically, as my tongue drilled into his deep hole to taste his well-hidden knot of skin.

His pitiful penis suffered throughout his ordeal. Thick meat throbbed against my chest attempting to free itself from my weighted prison. Surely his nuts also were pained, compacted by the weight of my chest and mass of his cock, but it was a pleasurable pain. John's silent raising of his chest and sinking of his belly invited more of it. He got plenty.

Eventually John's cock was released from bondage, but its freedom was short-lived. No sooner had it flipped onto his belly with the raising of my chest than did I bury it into my mouth.

Classroom skills put to good use, I crushed his perfectly shaped and sized dick, making my mouth a tight pussy for him – a pussy that did all the work, directed by a brain that remembered what he likes. Orgasms that interrupt one's sleep are hard to match. With John's mind still lingering in the subconscious where all fantasies come true, he injected me with a manly dose his seed.

"Jason, come up here with me," he softly instructed while still sprawled. As my chest met his and I laid atop him, John wrapped his arms across my back and squeezed tightly.

"I ain't ever lettin' you go." He nearly shouted, his mood bordering on anger when he repeated it. "You hear me? I ain't ever lettin' you go."

I struggled to speak, as his crushing bear hug made it very difficult to breath. "Don't worry... John... I'm... not... going anywhere."

"Damn right!" He viciously rolled us over and put himself on top, causing our bodies to nearly slip off the side of the bed. Keeping me firmly wrapped in his bear hug, he lifted me up and shifted me to the pillow, then slammed me down to the position he had just abandoned. With my chest cavity still clamped in his vise, John rapidly planted kisses all over my forehead, nose, cheeks and lips. My face was assaulted with frantic pecks, while my ribs were crushed between his chest and forearms.

I was manhandled. And I loved it.

Every part of me was a useless rag completely under his spell, except for my dick. It was fully charged and had been ever since I'd awakened atop his belly. And because John knew I loved his belly as much as he loved me loving it, he brought it into play in a manner unexpected.

John rose on his knees ever so slightly. With his arms still encircling my back and pressing our chests together, he slowly thrust himself forward, rubbing the head of my cock against the skin of his belly. Hard kisses relentlessly peppered my face. Powerful arms mercilessly crushed my chest, while John's erotically smooth and talented abdominal cavity masturbated me.

My hands clasped onto his back, racing up and down his undulating muscles, and although I said nothing, I thought plenty.

Oh, my god, you rough-ass son of a bitch... what the hell are you doing to me? God, your belly feels so good... so fucking soft... and hard... and just the right pressure... ooh... what the hell was that? OOH! There it is again... oh, geez... are you fuckin' kidding me? That's his belly button... ooh, god damn... it's clipping the head of my dick... ooh, shit... there it goes the other way... where the hell did you learn how to do this? Oh, man... there it is again... god, I can feel his tits scraping me too... you beautiful mother... ooh, that navel... skin's so tight... fuck an A... you talented piece of work, you... I can't believe this shit... beating me off with his god damned belly button... ooh, there it goes... oh, god damn, John... I love you... damn you to hell... I love you...

And at that moment I did love him. Would never say it though, even in the heated passion of a belly button jack off. Learned that one on my own. People say all sorts of silly things when they're busting a nut, and a man telling a married man that he loves him definitely qualifies as silly and useless. Besides, actions do speak louder than words, and John knew I was enamored with him. He had to know, just as I knew in my heart that he fancied me. Why else would a twenty year old and a forty year old take up with each other in the first place? What we had going here transcended age, marital status, and any other road block put in our way. The forces we had unleashed could only be fed with man juice, his and mine, and our elevated lust delivered what we needed when we needed it.

In one magical night, John gave so much of himself to me. His dick, balls and semen were all I expected, but John also gave me lessons in my young life, adventures never before available to me even in my wildest imagination. John showed me a world I never knew existed, a world I never wanted to leave.

After releasing me from his grip, John retrieved a towel to clean the humongous wad of sperm he had brought out of me, and then wet a cloth to wash away the sticky remnants from his belly and mine.

We put the pillows back to their proper position, turned out the light and resumed our slumber. This time it was permanent. I slept peacefully, resting my head in the crook of his arm until morning light caused him to stretch and announce that he had to piss. Typical John, he directed his stream to the center of the bowl, a masculine splashing of bravado to wake the dead.

"You play pool?"

"Not seriously."

"Ok, Jason. We'll find us a good table next week and go at it."

Only two words in that sentence registered with me – next week.

PART FIVE - ANGLES

Pete's Tavern became our Friday night watering hole because Pete's pool table was relatively new and never busy, nor was the rest of Pete's Tavern.

"The cue ball, Jason. It's all about the cue ball," John explained before breaking for our first-ever game of eight-ball. The next thing he said was, "eight in the side," as he ended the game with me never having moved, never having taken a single shot. Was John a smart-ass? Yes he was, but only for demonstration. Subsequent games had him missing on purpose so that he could explain what I'd done to miss from inability. First he helped me figure out the proper angles to sink the shot. Then he worked with me on english and speed to ensure I had a series of shots available, and the only reason I'm telling you this is because playing pool is a great way to meet people – if you catch my drift. In four years I don't think I ever legitimately took a game from him. My only wins came when he was either distracted or bored, but still, because of John I am pretty darned good compared to most.

Our routine was now established. Wednesday afternoons the rumble of John's cock shooting come into my mouth was matched only by the rumble of the elevator motor under him. Friday nights into Saturday mornings, the smacking of balls at Pete's was followed by the smacking of crotch to ass and mouth to cock by way of an all-nighter in our sleazy downtown hotel room, always enhanced by side-wall mirror.

Thing is, once word got out that Charlie and his gang had been replaced by John and his nephew, all the old regulars started returning to Pete's. Turns out the neighborhood wasn't so dead after all, as a plethora of working stiffs came in to unwind with no fear of bullies ruining their evening.

"Jack ain't much a business man," John told me. "Lettin' three bums run away his good customers."

"How come it took you so long to run 'em off, John?"

"Couldn't do it alone. Needed a partner."

Felt pretty good to hear him say that, but it only lasted a few seconds before he spoiled it. "Actually, I used to hang out here way back when. Hadn't been in for years, but a fella at work happened to mention coming to Pete's and the three goof balls stirring shit, so I decided to investigate."

"You planned to take 'em on all along?"

"Yep, but not with you. Our little discovery at Wilbert's just came along at the same time. I figured you wouldn't mind watching me whip their ass or at least die trying."

We really did try to stay out of trouble, but for whatever reason some guys were tempted to fuck with us. Sometimes it was because we couldn't be taken from the pool table until we were finished with it, but usually it was because too much beer had made them more brave than sensible. Sure, we could have chosen more upscale drinking establishments to avoid this, but John preferred to mingle with the muck. He never fooled me. John relished teasing the half-wits and they would always fall for his cocky strut, the price of which was our endless rain of fists. How could I not love a man whose chest preceded him with every step? John alone was enough to handle, but with my unimpressive stature appearing to pose no threat, those who dared challenge what we presented found to their dismay that together John and I were an unmovable force.

One day something happened that altered our schedule a bit. I was terminated from my employment. Although our date in the engine room technically was the cause of it, the real reason was that someone came along and stole a bunch of hats while I was busy working on John's motor. Security guards caught them at the door, but the security video tape clearly showed that the department was unmanned during the incident. So, when my boss asked me where I was at the time and my insistence that I was taking a shit didn't wash with video tape showing me coming out of the stock room, he decided my dishonesty made me unfit for this wonderful job. Funny, nothing was said about John's emergence from the same stock room not more than five minutes after mine. Maybe they stopped watching the tape after they saw me.

No matter, everything was good, because this persuaded me to do what I should have done much earlier, which was to confess to my parents that I hated school and probably was just wasting my time and their money. They didn't argue. Their son was not the same person who'd left podunk one year prior. Their Jason was instilled with a self-confidence that defied argument, and so my plans went forward unobstructed. I rented an apartment, which soon became a love pad, making it unnecessary for John and me to check into a sleazy hotel room. He took care of the mirror problem. From the very same Wilbert's Department Store where we first got acquainted, John purchased a handsome piece of five by four glass, also arranging and paying for its installation on my side wall at mattress level. Whether horizontal or vertical, John's performances were doubled for my pleasure.

With John's good word, his company overlooked my fall from grace at the department store. I got a job with Montgomery – not maintenance, but working on crews to install both elevators and escalators into new buildings. John set me up for life in so many ways.

We ran together for four good years, keeping our distance in the workplace. This was easy to do, since our paths rarely crossed other than for morning clock-ins and afternoon clock-outs, but when John had his accident word spread quickly amongst all employees.

He'd been charged with training a new hire, something he'd done many times before. During the third of five weeks' worth of instruction, John and the new man were working escalators in an office building very early in the morning. He'd told the trainee to go to the control room and turn off the circuits, and then alert the man at the main security desk that the escalators would be shut down for a couple of hours. For whatever reason, John removed the metal plate on the upper level and climbed down into the motor works before his trainee had put up the warning gates below. Not seeing John at the top, an office building maintenance employee flipped the switch at the bottom. Lo and behold, the circuit was active and both of John's legs were crushed just above his knees.

A hospital room is not the ideal situation in which to meet for the first time the wife of the man with whom you've been carrying on for four years. Rarely had he mentioned her to me. I'd always figured that as long as I could have him for twelve hours a week, the rest was hers. I did not need or want to know and he did not need or want to share.

Lydia McMurtry was her name. John had told me that, but little else about her or his life with her. My self-introduction, done in John's room as he lay sleeping nearby after his double-legged amputation, brought from her no expression of recognition, so if she ever before had heard John mention my name she either didn't remember or was a very good actress.

"So, Jason, do you work with John?"

"We've never worked together, but John got me on with Montgomery's installation crew. I first met him when I worked at Wilbert's over on 74th Street."

"Oh, I see."

"The elevator motor was in my stock room. John always took time to stop and talk to me before doing his maintenance back there."

"He does have the gift of gab."

"He's just a good person, Mrs. McMurtry. I want you to know that I'm pulling for him. All of us are."

"Thank you, Jason. We appreciate that. Probably in a couple of days he'll be up wanting someone to talk to besides me, so I hope you'll stop by for a visit."

"I sure will, Mrs. McMurtry. You tell him I said hello."

It came as no surprise that John himself called me the very next evening.

"Jason, get your ass over here."

He was weak, but still managed to instill his usual bravado while telling the tale of his chopping. He planned to approach this setback as he had all things in life, with cocky confidence and no consideration for the possibility of defeat. John insisted that I come visit him every day.

"And when I get home, I might need you to help Lydia get me in and out of my wheelchair every now and then, until I learn how to do it myself."

"All you gotta do is call me. I'll come running."

"You better. If you ever want to see this again." He pointed to his gown-covered penis, relishing my look of curiosity. "Yes, it still works, best I can tell. I'll be needing you to test that out, too."

Risky business that, but I guess no more than doing it in the stock room of Wilbert's Department Store. Two nights later we tried it. Lydia left at seven. John called me at seven-o-one. I arrived at seven-thirty-six, and just like our first time in John's little motor room, he told me what to do.

"Close that door and lock it."

"Uh, John... this door doesn't lock."

"Well, close it and prop a chair back to it. My dick's too important for my rough hand job."

He threw back the covers while I secured the door. I overlooked his bandaged stumps, but by this time much of John's personality had rubbed off on me, so I made light of his situation.

"Sure am gonna miss your pretty legs and feet."

"Well, tough shit. You had plenty of opportunities."

"Yeah, and I took 'em, too... didn't I?"

"Got that right, Jason. Now, get busy and see if this thing works."

I'll say one thing, getting John's boxers off of him took a lot less effort. Did it work? John's cock was halfway inflated when my mouth made it disappear. It ballooned to full strength just like always and my experience with it told me he was about ready to blow when a damned nurse tried to enter the room. I spit him out.

"What do you want me to do?"

"Ah, fuck it. Let 'em in. I'll never get off with them banging on the door."

We were admonished for our make-shift door lock, I more than he, and although I'm sure nurse what's her name knew exactly what we'd been doing, John's perfectly put back together garments kept her guessing.

After she left, John had lost his mood, figuring it would only happen again right when he was getting close to explosion.

"I think we've answered our question, Jason. I'll see if I can't finish myself later tonight. Sure breaks my heart having to do it that way."

It was tough not having access to him in the ways I needed. But John did make good progress and I figured it was just a matter of time before he came up with a way for me to worship him again. My assistance at his home was needed but for his first two days. Lydia was present for both. Once John got situated and adapted to life with no legs, he insisted I come for weekly Friday night visits. Tradition, you know. Lydia was present for those, too, but at this point just being in the same room with John was enough for me.

Feigning kitchen duties, Lydia kindly gave us time alone.

"Jason, don't get pissed off at me," John warned. "But my wife fucked me the other night."

"Why would that piss me off? I think that's what you oughtta be doing."

"Yeah. Had to fuck up. She did all the work."

"And did it work?"

"Yeah, buddy... like a charm."

"I'd kiss you if I could. Here." I kissed my fingers and slapped his cheek. "Traitor."

"Ha... sorry... she came first. Don't you worry. I'll get better, then we'll figure something out. Think you can handle half a man?"

"Are you kidding? I already conquered the whole. Now I can really torture you. You'll be helpless to run away from me."

"Just like I always was."

Losing both legs never changed John one bit. He still looked for good times from a new perspective, but even tough guys like John can only take so many punches. Once he returned to the hospital with an infection, John was no more. His eyes were dead, his bravado gone, and my heart sank when I entered his room to see it. With Lydia there John put up a fairly good front. After she left for the evening John spoke to me as a defeated man.

"It ain't no good, Jason."

"I know, John. It's hard to tell a good story when you can't move around."

"You got that right. Can't kick a man's ass without feet." He threw back the covers to see what was no longer there. "Funny, feels like I still got 'em." This was spoken with voice inflection dull, nearly mono-tone. Those always upturned corners of his mouth had reversed direction.

His stumps were heavily bandaged, some sort of yellowish fluid seeping to stain them. "Are you in pain, John?"

"Ha, I'm hurtin' all over... I'd just as soon get out of here and go home."

"Then go home, John."

He turned with a look serious and sad. "Die there instead of here... is that it?"

"If you're not happy where you are, move." I grabbed his meaty hand and squeezed. "Those are your words, not mine, way back when I's at Wilbert's. Remember?"

"I also told you I'd never let you go. Guess I was wrong about that."

"No you weren't." I leaned close, ran my fingers through his scalp, tousled my Navy man's hair, kissed his anchor-tattooed forearm. "Let's just reverse it, John. I'm never letting you go. Doesn't matter what you do. Everything we've done, everything you've taught me, that can never be taken from me." I lifted his gown, rubbed his belly. "And when I need you again... and I *will* need you again... I know you'll be around, so don't worry about it. Do what you gotta do."

"Kiss me, god damn it."

"Where?"

He tapped his well-covered peter with his index finger about the same time a nurse entered his room. She took his vital signs, updated his chart, and left without speaking to either one of us, at which time I chair-jammed the door good and hard. We didn't bother removing his boxers. I did him through the slit.

"If you get me, don't swallow, Jason... probably poison."

The angle was wrong, but John had taught me all about angles. I got him and I kept him, poison or no. It took John much more time than I'd remembered, and at least two nurses were banging the door when he fired his load. It was worth the wait, a long time coming for both of us. As I tucked away John's perfect pecker moisture framed his eyes, but those mouth corners were once again turned in my direction. The

180

single tear that finally trickled was for good reason.

"Here, now," I collected that tear with my index finger, licked that index finger. "No tough guy of mine's gonna be seen crying... not by anyone but me."

Was it worth my reprimand from hospital staff and permanent banishment from his room? Damned straight it was. My next evening's phone call came from Lydia, not John. She informed me of his passing. With great effort, I held my shit together until they dropped him into the ground, although the heart-wrenching ceremonies of full-military honors were hard to take. My crying session was done in private on my bed with our mirror staring back at me. That piece of glass has traveled with me on my every move from one residence to another, and to this day it is properly mounted as per his instructions.

These days John holds on loosely, but we've never let go. He's part of my intuition. He's my warning signals, alerting me with those helpful voices that say, "something's not right here... don't do it;" or "this person's bad news... stay away."

Maybe you believe such things and maybe you don't, but it works for me and that's all that matters. I'm sure that John is still teaching others how to get the most out of life, sharing with them his "don't give a shit" approach to it all. With his guidance, I still do things the Navy John way. That man will always bring out the best of me.

ABOUT THE AUTHOR

Jardonn Smith is the instigator of the BDSM web site Jardonn's Erotic Tales.com, where you'll also find the audio MP3 erotica of his Uncle Jasper and writings of cousin Jack. Together, the three of them tell their adventures of straight, gay and bisexual activities.

Jardonn sees his men as god-like, heroic creatures, and he insists they be bound to their altars in order to receive his praise. It is the only proper method in which to glorify the beauty of the male physique.

Jardonn Smith is also the author of:

I'll Never Talk: Erotic Tales of Defiant Men
The Bishop of Grunewald: A Tale from the Dungeon
Liquid Delights: Erotic Tales of Wetness

Available at Goodboner.com or jardonnserotictales.com

www.ingramcontent.com/pod-product-compliance
Lightning Source LLC
Chambersburg PA
CBHW071214260626
47162CB00004B/1290